THE ANTUNITE CHRONICLES: BOOK 1

TERRY BIRDGENAW

While reading this book, you will come to know historical arthropod fictional figures whose names, words, or actions may resemble people here on Earth, either from the present or past. The resemblance is only implied for humoristic purposes and is not meant to reflect literal, thematic, or chronologic historical accuracy, as the novel epitomizes political satire or parody. Except for public or famous historical figures whose statements appeared in the public domain, any resemblance of the insect and insectoid characters to persons living or dead is coincidental. The views and opinions expressed by these rhyming insects, or the insectoid historian narrator, are their own and should not be attributed to the author.

ISBN: 978-1-7781516-0-6 (paperback)

ISBN: 978-7781516-1-3 (ebook)

Legal deposit, Library and Archives Canada, May 2022

*This book is dedicated to the victims of the invasion
of Ukraine by Russian aggressors, and casualties
in all wars throughout human history.*

MAPS AND CHARTS

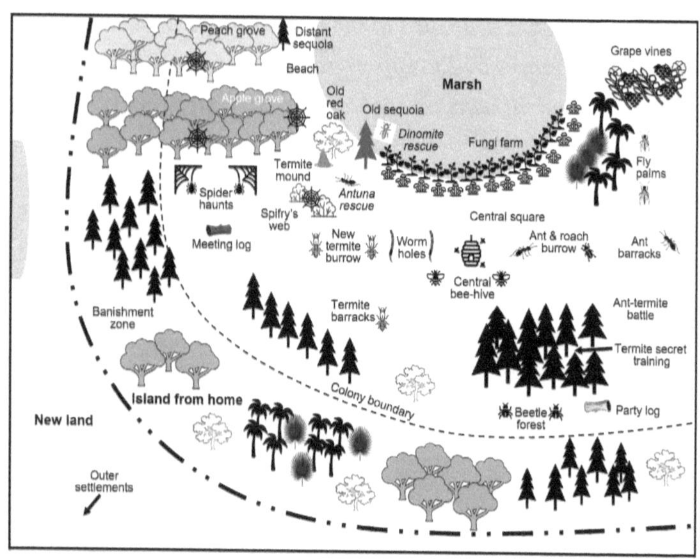

MAP OF POO-PONIC'S FIRST COLONY

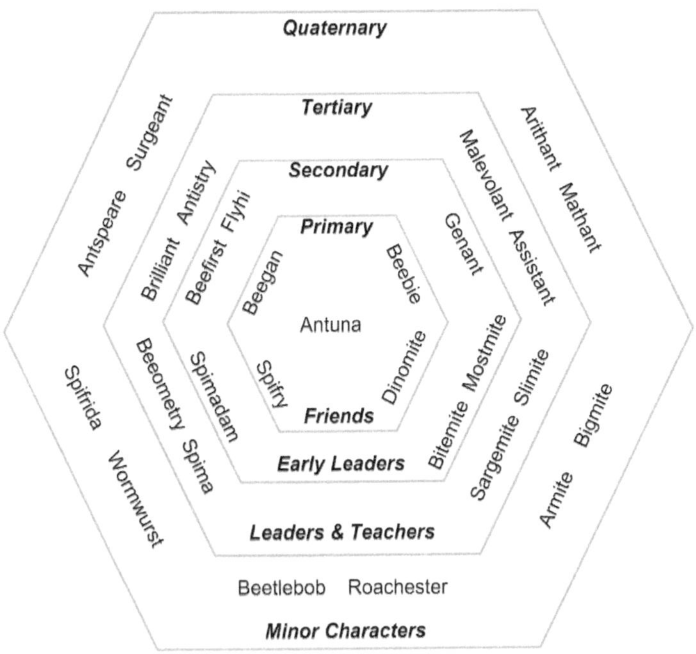

CHARACTER HIVE FOR ANTUNA'S STORY

PROLOGUE

Yucatan Peninsula, Earth, late Cretaceous period (~65 million years B.C.)

THE LONG GRASS swayed in the gentle breeze, casting a shimmering picket fence-like silhouette that dappled the bright sunlight from the parched ground. A small ant appeared to struggle very little while carrying a deceased wasp on her back across the sward-covered plain. The solar light piercing through the wasp's translucent wings intensified the hues of the ant's caramel-colored cranium, thorax, and shiny, licorice-black abdomen. The wasp's glassy sails magnified the candy apple-red flecks splattered across the ant's thorax, giving her a distinctive glow.

Out of nowhere, a threatening termite challenged her for the quarry, and six of the ant's comrades appeared to encourage its retreat. A spider witnessed the encounter on overhanging arid sagebrush, but since he had recently devoured an enormous meal, his interest waned, and he returned to weaving his spiraling web. Further overhead, two honeybees flew by, buzzing to each other on their good fortune that they were not the objects of the pall-bearing ant. While fixated on the departed wasp, the bees needed to veer their course to avoid a flying swarm of houseflies headed south, following the pungent aroma of a decaying mouse carcass calling them to breakfast. Due west, a possi of wood-boring beetles gnawed through a broken but live sequoia limb, tasting the sweet sap as ample sawdust littered the meadow floor. As the litter rained down, roaches rustling in a bed of dried leaves below indulged in the free buffet falling upon them and bouncing off their slippery shells. The ant vibrated and stumbled when an earthworm surfaced from an underground expedition next to her. Unfazed by the tremor, the ant continued along her way.

In the surrounding hectares, countless other scenes like this mirrored the ant's journey in the complex yet unsophisticated intertwining of insect life. But a few hexutes before the ant arrived at her nest, as the bees neared their hive and the flies only moments before had reached their scavenged feast, it happened. A powerful force ripped rhododendrons and fledgling apple trees from their loamy moorings. Coconuts and green cones were heaved like metal shards drawn to a powerful magnet. The gravitational energy pulled honey-laden beehives as a vacuum cleaner sucks dust bunnies into its bagged belly. Termite-filled deadwood was tossed like flotsam sailing towards a broken shore on hurricane-lashed waves. With a deafening boom, the turbulence gobbled up insects, grasses, plants, and soil for miles around, like a tornado drawing shoddily constructed dwellings towards the heavens. Then, as fast as it began, it was over.

Without understanding their fate, a group of Earth insects was displaced from their comfortable habitat to a new reality on a planet they never knew existed. They did not choose to migrate to an unknown world—this life-changing event was thrust upon them. The story of the small wasp-laden ant, Antuna, is only known because she barely survived the wormhole passage. Her descendants kept a pheromonal history of the account on Earth and what followed. The insects later recorded the story with chemical structures for their pheromonics, written either on clay tablets or papyrus. Below is the tale of Antuna's arrival and survival, what she remembered, and what her new friends told her. The account taught us a lot about the insects' ancient history on their new planet—their struggles, growing pains, accomplishments, and how circumstances realized or squashed their dreams.

OPENING PODCAST [INTERVIEW]

Vive: This is Vive McDougall with my weekly Astro-science read-u-mentary podcast, *What's Out There?* [momentary pause] It's September 3, 2050, and our first show of the new season. For new listeners, this is a podcast where we interview Astro-science fact and science fiction authors about their books and read excerpts or chapters from them. Our goal is to excite listeners about breakthroughs in the astronomical sciences and learn more about our society through an intense examination of science fiction [00:31]. And folks, we have a treat for you today! Actually, you're in for an entire bag of goodies because the read-u-mentary podcast that starts today will last several weeks since it's so fascinating that we could not cram it all into one or two sessions. These podcasts are going to be a little different from usual. First, the author we're interviewing is a historian, not an Astro-scientist or science fiction writer. And he comes from, wait for it [pause] another galaxy! [laughs] [01:00] Second, our guest has agreed that we can read his entire book because of its phenomenal significance. We will read a chapter from his book each week and interview him today and after the last chapter. Yes indeed, we have with us, well remotely, or I should say very remotely, Narrant, the famous historian from the moon of our sister planet, Bilaluna. He's been the talk of planet Earth ever since we learned he'd be releasing the first book in his series, *The Complete History of Poo-ponic and Bilaluna: Part one–Antuna's Story*. [01:31] [short pause] Welcome, Narrant, or should I call you Professor?

Narrant: Narrant is fine. After all, the people and insectoids from our two worlds have become so friendly since we first met.

Vive: Narrant, I am thrilled to read your manuscript on our podcast because the history you have written is so detailed, and our listeners are eager to learn about it. Most we know about your planet and moon is based on rumors and the bits of information released by NASA and other space organizations. [01:58] We know that your insect society went through an enormous upheaval when you left Earth and traveled through the wormhole, and now we will all hear about it. But first, tell our listeners a little about you.

Narrant: I am a cyborg insect or insectoid known as an ANT, for allied noble tripod, the first cyborg insect phylogenetic family created on Poo-ponic. I live along with 999 other insectoids on Bilaluna, Poo-ponic's moon. We are descendants of the colonists that came to Bilaluna from Poo-ponic 15,000 hexs ago. [02:30]

Vive: Narrant, I hope you don't mind if I sometimes interrupt for clarification. Please explain to our listeners what a hex is. Or should I say—What the hex? [laughs]

Narrant: We use a heximal counting system as insects have six limbs. I created words for you like hexonds and hexades using hex as the root of all time units to show they're heximal, and each step goes up by X6, not X10.

Vive: I saw you have an appendix in your book which explains this.

Narrant: Yes, I used the decimal system for most numbers, but as a historian, I wanted to retain our own system for time units. [3:03]

Vive: Let's get back to you, Narrant, and your book. Could you give our listening audience a little more background about your engaging society, how you evolved, and why you wrote your books?

Narrant: Vive, our first colonists were refugees from Poo-ponic, where our small biological insect ancestors first constructed cyborg insects. To avoid the cultural and environmental mistakes of our past and to provide a caution to our new friends on Earth, the All-insect Historical Society or AHS deemed it time to record the history of Poo-ponic and Bilaluna. [03:35]

Vive: That seems like a tall order. Had you any reservations at first?

Narrant: Absolutely. I found myself staring into my telescreen and down at my claw pad. I dreaded scratching the chemical formulae one by one with the two claws on each of my forelegs for the task given to me.

Vive: Please explain what you mean by chemical formulae.

Narrant: Well, ants communicate with each other and other insects using pheromones, and we must use strings of chemical formulae to write down our sentences. I first inscribed my book in what we call 'pheromonics.' [04:04]

Vive: You use a syntax generator that your scientists developed to translate 'pheromonics' into English?

Narrant: That's correct. But I also had to probe deeply into human civilization, so I could make references and analogies that you would recognize. I am what we call an amateur humanologist.

Vive: That is an exciting approach, and the story is remarkable. Could you tell our listeners what period of your history the first volume covers?

Narrant: This volume extends from the arrival of our insect ancestors on Poo-ponic to the end of the Spider and Termite war. It is our ancient history. [04:40]

Vive: I see that the story, as all histories are, is about your

    Terry Birdgenaw

people, or should I say insects, and how they coped. You have such detail, even from mega-years ago.

Narrant: Yes, the treatise follows the tales of great and infamous insects and cyborgs, including one of our first colonists, Antuna, the first Queen bee, Beefirst, and the warrior ants Genant, Malevolant, and Antistry. This first volume follows a detailed pheromonal record, like human oral histories, kept by Antuna's descendants. [05:07] It reflects her time growing up. So, it allowed me to write this history, at times more like a story.

Vive: I loved the parts about Antuna and her friends and how they facilitated the early survival of insects on the planet. Are those true stories?

Narrant: Yes, but I dramatized them to flesh out the details. I changed the names since I could not translate them from pheromones to any intelligible English words. They always start or finish with the character's species to make it easy for you. [05:30] I often used the rest of the moniker to reflect their position or physical characteristics, so I could keep them straight. Sometimes, I used a name because I thought it was funny.

Vive: So, you called your character Beefirst because she was the first queen bee on Poo-ponic?

Narrant: Exactly, and I named Antuna with the Spanish word 'una' after 'ant' because she was the first ant described in the book.

Vive: Ah, very clever, and Spanish too.

Narrant: Well, I am a historian, so I tried to acquire as much knowledge about Earth as I could. [06:01] Some names reflect famous people in your past. This book is not only translated, but it is also a version targeted to you—insectoids would not understand many references.

Vive: And your history is so rich. It seems your society went through an incredible evolution, one that you might say parallels human history.

Narrant: That's true. This first book records momentous events throughout our past, including our early survival on Poo-ponic, intellectual evolution, and struggles between species. [06:31]

Vive: Indeed, your account seems like a roller-coaster ride of highs and lows.

Narrant: Well, it was not all gloom and doom. Some parts were heartening, some were humorous, and there was hope.

Vive: I enjoyed the balance of tragedy and comedy. There was such misfortune, but I sometimes laughed aloud while discovering it. And poetry before every chapter, that's quite unusual for a history book.

Narrant: As a historian, my account was as accurate as possible. [07:00] However, I reserved the right to make poetic preludes to each chapter to acknowledge my rhyming ancestors.

Vive: Wait, did you say rhyming ancestors? What do you mean?

Narrant: It goes back to one of our early poets, Antspeare, a poor but wise ant. His poems were very popular—he was a little like your own Dr. Seuss. Yet his poems were not for children but for adults.

Vive: Antspeare [laughing] that's a good one. And I am guessing he influenced how insects spoke?

Narrant: Yes, Antspeare had an adage about good insect speech: [07:31] *'It won't ring my chimes if it ain't got no rhymes!'* But ironically, it was the elites in the society that took up what we dubbed Antspearean speech. Most ordinary insects didn't bother with it unless they wanted to make a statement.

Vive: I see you broke your history up into two books. Why is that?

Narrant: Each book covers a vital part of our history, with mega-hexs separating them. In between, we either have little information, or not much of great significance occurred. [07:59]

Vive: And what would you say to our listeners about why they should read this book? I assume you wish to highlight the struggles between aggression and altruism.

Narrant: Yes, [in a severe tone] other civilizations should learn from the error of our ways.

Vive: Our leaders have also steered us down the wrong path, and our world is worse off for it. And with that, we should start with the first chapter.

Narrant: I am excited to share our story with Earthlings.

Vive: Okay, listeners, let's begin. Every podcast will present a chapter—each one starting with Narrant's lovely poems. [08:34] Our chapter readings will go week-by-week until we finish the six chapters. Narrant will join us at the end of this volume for another interview to sum things up.

Narrant: You flatter me too much, Vive.

Vive: And by the way, listeners, as with all our podcasts, you can either listen each week on Saturday or read the clean verbatim transcripts uploaded the next day. Here goes—*The Complete History of Poo-ponic and Bilaluna: Part one—Antuna's Story* by our guest Narrant. [09:00]

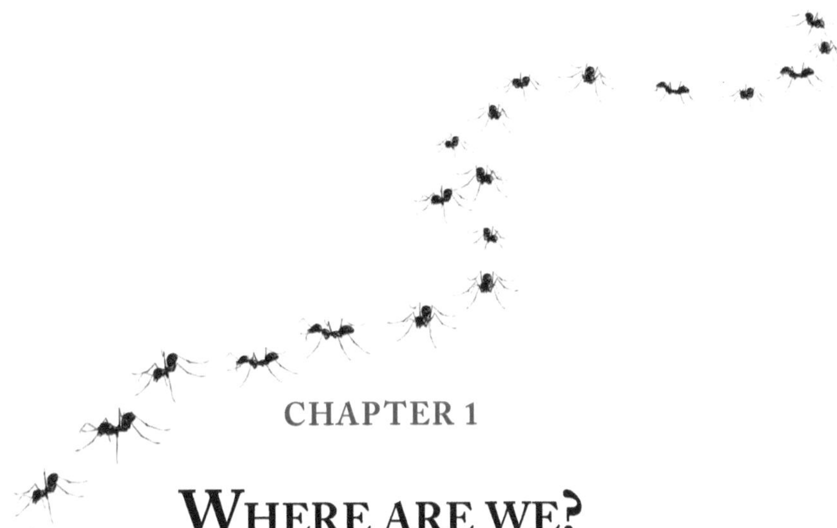

CHAPTER 1

WHERE ARE WE?

*A marooning like a bolted hatch can
unfasten portholes to a new sphere.*

*And what is the island on that frontier? But
terrain that engulfs one's eye as it juts out
in the vast sea of its new atmosphere.*

**Unknown planet, 23.03 billion light-hexs away from Earth,
moments after the Prologue.**

BEEGAN FOUND HERSELF several hundred feet from her broken-down hive, grounded and covered in dirt but otherwise unhurt. Another honeybee, Beebie, arose first, shaking the soil off her silky wings.

"Hey, watch that shaking. You're burying me alive here!" Beegan called out from under a nearby pile of soil, releasing a ragged reek. *I feel so cranky I'm losing it.*

Beebie stopped shuttering and leaped away from the dirt pile. "Sorry, Sis, I didn't see you there. Are you okay?"

"Yes, if I could see any light." Beegan fluttered her wings to dust off, lacking her usual grace. "What the heck happened?" Shaking off the dirt, she revealed her sleek body, which mirrored her identical twin sister. Her slender head had large compound eyes on each side that dominated the oblong spheroid. Her hairy skull was perched atop a fuzzy, mellow yellow thorax, affixed to a shiny, hairless, ebony, gold striped abdomen. Glossy, translucent wings extended from her fluffy middle almost to the end of her bulbed rear tip.

"I don't know, Sis. Maybe it was an earthquake," surmised Beebie.

Beegan twirled, trying to get her bearings. *How can I not know where I am? I'm usually so grounded.* "Could be, but look over there," she said. "Where did that water come from?"

"Is it a marsh?" questioned Beebie.

Beegan hovered closer to the waterhole, as perplexed as a bee trying to get nectar from plastic flowers. "I guess so, but there are no lily pads. The algae are so thick—you can't tell how deep the marsh is." *No matter how long I look at it, I can't figure out what has happened.*

"Yes, some of this scene looks like our home. But a lot seems strange."

Pulling at her antennae, Beegan scanned the landscape in all directions. "Wow, Beebie, I got a feeling we're not in Laramidia anymore!"

Indeed, the bee sisters were transplanted to a new planet when a giant meteorite strike on Earth opened a wormhole, causing several thousand insects to transit to a faraway galaxy. The intense energy from the approaching meteorite caused an enormous alteration in the area's magnetic field. The force stretched cosmic strings and enlarged an existing subatomic wormhole to a size able to transport living beings. The gravitational energy drew enough stabilizing exotic matter to uphold the portal, which would otherwise collapse. The attractive forces also sucked large amounts of flora and fauna into the gateway. They transported the portal to a planet in a spiral galaxy, 23.03 billion light hexs away from Earth. You could say the wormhole beamed the bees up.

Beegan continued to question where they were, emitting a fuzzy fragrance. "Beebie, it couldn't have been an earthquake. A quake wouldn't pull us out of the air like that." Squinting, she pointed to the sky where they were moments before.

Beebie hovered off the ground, beating her wings on one side, then twirled herself like a top. "Maybe it was a twister. But I didn't see any cone clouds. And there wasn't much wind."

Beegan snatched Beebie, yanking her back to the ground. "This is no time for your antics!" Then she heaved and glanced up. "A twister draws things up, but this jerked us down. Whatever it was, it was strange."

"Do you think alien insects abducted us and took us to their planet far away?" questioned Beebie with a half-hearted hypothesis.

Beebie sometimes has fantastical ideas, but I know she can't be serious. "No way, alien insects are only mayfly stories, but this place is definitely alien." *Good thing she can lean on my rational nature.*

The force that brought them down was not as disruptive as a twister since much of the material sucked through came in a large swath, and most elements kept their structural connectivity with surrounding matter. Some plants, shrubs, and small trees were uprooted entirely, but most arrived intact, fixed in their earthly soil. It was like a mile-wide front-end loader had scooped out a chunk of the Earth's surface and roughly deposited it on another planet. Although some trees remained behind, those that passed through were often well-entrenched. The effect on plant life was much like what would have happened if it had endured a moderate earthquake. One could say shaken but not overly stirred.

For some unknown reason, animals from this period on Earth did not fare so well. Birds, dinosaurs, and mammals in the area did not pass through the wormhole and did not survive the devastation caused by the meteorite impact. Thus, the event only transported a minuscule cross-section of the invertebrate world. It was unclear why only eight animal species survived and landed safely on Poo-ponic. The surviving species included six families of *Insecta* (Formica, 'spraying' ants, common house flies, honey bees, roaches, wood-boring beetles, and termites), a species of the genus *Lumbricus* (earthworms), and one class of *Arachnida* (Scytodes, 'spitting' spiders). Even though these species survived, many individual creatures died on that hexay as burrows collapsed, hives flew, and the wormhole passage induced a shock that the weaker insects could not withstand.

A diminutive spider named Spifry watched from his frayed web as the bee sisters came into view. The early morning solar light cast a bulky, looming shadow that belied his tiny frame. A miniature bat-like face, dwarfed by protruding fangs, extended from his coppery cephalothorax, the base for eight gangly legs. An overly slender, mocha-colored abdomen highlighted his runty growth. He observed the bees approaching a petite ant that did not look like she would survive the trauma associated with the wormhole transit. He eavesdropped on their conversation.

"Hey, Sis, isn't that the ant we saw earlier carrying the dead wasp?" asked Beebie.

Spifry watched Beegan intently, edging toward the prone ant. He heard her say to her sister, "Yes, and she doesn't look too good. What can we do?"

While many bees and spiders would not care about the fate of another insect, the strange circumstances instilled a 'we're in this together' sensibility that pre-empted normal aggressive or defensive instincts. *I could spring out of my web and aid the bees, but they're bees.*

Antuna lay in the dirt and appeared to be in shock. She convulsed violently hexonds later.

Spifry froze while watching Beebie hover over the tiny ant.

"Oh my, she's shuddering!" she said. "I think she stopped breathing!"

Spifry's impulse to assist intensified, like the urge to build an extra web during a locust swarm. *I'll just wait and see what the bees do.*

He saw Beegan shaking her head from side to side. "Looks like her heart stopped," she said. "There's nothing we can do."

He curtailed catapulting out of his web and listened further.

"What if I sting her?" Beebie said, hovering over the dying ant. "I can restart her little heart."

Spifry snickered. *I can't imagine a bee stinging an ant.*

"That would kill her double, and you might rip out your guts trying," she said.

Spifry had never spoken to a bee before. *I should mind my own business.* Yet he heeded as Beebie pleaded further, "But what can we do? We can't let her die before our eyes."

Beegan dumbfounded Spifry when she gazed upon him, calling out, "Hey spider boy, can you come here and help us out?"

What? No bee or any other insect had ever asked me for help before. Spifry cautiously slunk down from his web, discharging a vague vapor. "I guess so. What can I do?"

Beegan motioned to the now limp ant with a glare. "This young ant's heart just stopped. Can you use a bit of venom to get it going again?"

Spifry advanced warily but snorted when he heard Beebie say, "Won't his toxin be too strong?"

"Nah, it could work. You can see I'm kinda small," Spifry blurted. "It often takes a few bites to kill my prey." *But I can't believe I am telling you that.*

Spifry approached the now motionless ant while Beegan implored, "Then do it. She's dying!"

Spifry straddled the ant, but before giving her a bite, he said, "Okay, okay, but only this once. I don't want the guys knowing I helped bees and ants."

A tense silence followed, as the bite didn't appear to work. Beebie stooped down to check the ant's heart. "Nothing's happening. Bite her again!"

Spifry stood up and scowled at Beebie. "Wait, it takes time! First, it will stun her, and then the pain should shock her out of it." He explained further, "She just needs to pump a little hemolymph up to her brain." *I haven't killed many, but I know what my venom can do.*

Sure enough, the flaccid ant at first went quite stiff but jolted from her deadly sleep a few hexonds later.

Despite his accurate forecast, Antuna startled Spifry when she jumped up and cried, "Ouch, did you just bite me?"

Spifry leaped back, alarmed, after Antuna kicked him and cocked her sprayer. *Whoa, I've heard that stuff is deadly.*

Beegan sprung between them, "Wait, don't spray him. He saved your life. Your heart stopped."

Spifry gasped and relaxed like a monarch butterfly finishing its long migration. "You sure have some kick in you now, though," he said.

The two bee sisters praised Spifry for his life-saving act, and they introduced themselves. Despite her near-death experience, Antuna was quite animated, and her anger dissipated quickly. Although these insects and the spider were recently post-pupal and young like human adolescents, they understood insect life is fragile. To them, death was a common thing and not so alarming. Therefore, they were often willing to risk their lives to save another, particularly their own kind, not fearing death. Antuna's sisters and brothers endangered themselves by building bridges or rafts with their bodies so that their queen and colony mates could cross divides or streams. Beegan and Beebie's siblings and cousins often sacrificed themselves to protect the hive. Even though they were the bee team, their best was top-notch. The tragic circumstances expanded altruistic tendencies, motivating different species to assist each other. Antuna thanked Spifry for saving her life.

Spifry retorted, "Don't thank me. It was the bees' idea. I only did what I do. And by the way, don't spread this around." *The guys would tease me to death, or a soldier might bite off my head for aiding the enemy.*

Yet, Spifry got a warm feeling when Antuna extended her antennae and tentatively touched his pedipalps in a friendly gesture. He cared less about what the other spiders thought, after all.

All we know of the early environment on the planet comes from the stories Antuna told about exploring with her new friends. After Antuna's miraculous recovery, the four pals surveyed their new surroundings to uncover where they were and what had changed. Soon they approached the area from the slice of Earth where the story began. Invigorated by her second chance at life, Antuna was excited to have friends from different insect families and an arachnid. Her heart warmed, sensing their pheromones and interacting with them as they explored their new surroundings.

"Beebie, you're right that things here look familiar," noted Beegan, while they strolled toward the marsh. "Look over there. That's the apple tree next to our last hex's beehive."

"I remember that sequoia tree—it still has its broken limb," noted Antuna. "It was full of beetles when I passed it earlier. Are they still there?" *I might have been out, but my memories from Earth are still as vivid as ever.*

Beebie took a short flight to scan the tree. "Yes, they're still boring away. Nothing ever fazes them."

Indeed, wood-boring beetles were the beavers or lumberjacks of their time. They worked hard and were always busy and undisturbed—even if their actions took down a large timber.

Antuna watched as Spifry crawled over for a closer look and instinctively spat at something rustling within the leaves beneath. Unperturbed by the attack, a massive roach yanked at the end of his spitting thread and pulled Spifry head over claw.

Antuna chuckled as the angry roach grumbled, "Geesh, can't a guy have a good meal anymore without interruptions?"

She helped Spifry to his feet as the cockroach stared at

Spifry and continued, "Earthquakes, spider attacks—you are a spider, right? Though I wouldn't know from that pathetic spit you threw."

"Sorry, sir, my instincts got the better of me. I'm not even hungry," Spifry apologized. Antuna dusted him off, and he retracted his spitting strands.

They both scuttled back to their friends, and Antuna smirked at them. "Wow, what a grroach."

Antuna perused the landscape beyond the marsh, spreading a shimmering scent. "A lot of our old neighborhood seems to be here, but it looks like an island from home, sitting on a sea of rock and dust."

Their new planet was one-tenth the size of Earth with a proportional reduction in gravity. Its atmosphere, water, and mineral content were like Earth's, and despite its barren look, Antuna's new planet was primed for the spread of vegetation throughout the land. It might have taken a few more hexuries to get going, but the transplanting of Earth's plants and insects sped up the process. The meteorite struck at the peak of early angiosperm pollen plants on Earth, and many flowering plants with seeds, pollen, and nectar came along. This little slice of Earth, or the 'island from home' as Antuna called it, ensured the insects' survival on the new planet. It was not yet a paradise, but they had their milk and honey, though they had to slog to keep it.

🐜 🐜 🐜

Antuna's island wasn't embedded in a sea as most are, but the large, displaced chunk of Earth crashed right next to one of the new planet's marshes. Fascinated but intimidated by the large waterhole, Antuna's friends approached it cautiously. Antuna herself marveled at her new surroundings as wide-eyed as a nanitic or young post-pupal ant emerging from its cocoon. It puzzled her that her friends were not more thrilled.

"What was that?" shrieked Beebie, responding to a loud succession of crack, thump, and splash sounds right behind them.

"Look," cried Beegan. "That bough has broken off, and some of it dropped into the water." She looked around for other falling branches. They were all jumpy.

Antuna tried to calm everyone. "I guess our beetle friends have finally eaten through it." *I've never faced such a crazy morning.*

She watched as Spifry raised his pedipalps to gauge the wind's direction. "It's blustery too," he said. "It overwhelmed the old tree, especially after the tremors and the displacement."

"Seems like the beetles are okay," Beegan noted. "Only half of the limb went into the water."

Antuna saw the smaller shoots slipping under the dark blue-green water and grew alarmed herself. "Wait, are those termites in the water?" *I think they're going to drown.*

"I see them," Beebie chimed in. "Three crawled onto that twig coming out of the water." They all watched the termites scurry up the branch before its end sank underwater.

"Oh, dear!" Antuna squirted an antsy aroma. "There's one still in the water, and there are no sprigs near him." Despite her earlier calming influence, Antuna scrambled toward the water's edge. *I must save him.*

"Don't worry. He'll swim to the shore." What Beegan said did not assure Antuna.

Instead, Antuna flailed her forelimbs, mimicking the termite's distress. "The wind is pushing the termite further out," she panted.

"It's only a termite Tune. I thought you ants hated them anyway," said Spifry.

Antuna fumed, but Spifry accurately identified ants' normal feelings for termites who often competed with them for food.

She glared at Spifry. "Look, you saved me, even though another time you'd have eaten me," she scolded. "What if it were you out there?" *We have to do something!*

Antuna grabbed a small twig from the fallen branch and then plunged into the water to rescue the termite. "I'll swim out to him. When I get there, Spifry, you spit at me and reel us both in." She gave Spifry a do-it-or-else look.

Antuna continued to stare at Spifry as he cautioned, "I can try, but it will sting a lot. It may stun you, so you can't swim."

Antuna softened her glare. "Look, Spifry, no insult intended, but your venom's not that strong." *Anyway, I'm going.*

Antuna overlooked Spifry when she noticed Beegan flying to the shoreline.

"Wait, you can't swim that far," warned Beegan. "Let me grab you and fly you over to him."

Beegan snatched tiny Antuna and flew her to the termite, whose limbs were flailing about as he slipped under the water. She hovered, then plopped Antuna next to him. Antuna used her lower limbs to grasp the sinking termite while clutching onto the twig with her upper limbs.

"Okay, I got him." Antuna hauled him up onto the twig. "Now Spifry spit at me and tug us back to shore." *He saved me before, and I know he'll come through.*

Spifry spat at her, but a gust of wind drove Antuna and the termite out of range. His thread missed them by inches.

"Again, Spifry! Try again!" Antuna wailed while the pair drifted farther out of reach.

"It's no use," cried Spifry. "You're too far. You'll have to swim."

Antuna despaired, but Beegan, who still hovered near her, buoyed her when she called out, "Beebie, get over here. Together, we can push them."

Beebie observed the ordeal from the shore and snapped to attention when Beegan called. She zoomed to the rescue site with steadfast determination. She and Beegan flapped their wings like chopper blades, churning up the water. Antuna sagged with exhaustion and let the bee sisters take control. They thrust her and the termite with their claws, rippling the water with their wingbeats. The deadweight of Antuna and the termite caused resistance, and the wind gusted against them. Antuna kicked to help but could only paddle her two rear legs, as she needed to grasp both the twig and the termite with the other four.

As they progressed, Spifry gauged their distance relative to his maximum spit range and bellowed, "You're in reach now. Get set!"

Antuna shut her eyes, anticipating the hit. She heard Spifry spit, but she felt no blow or sting. *He missed, and I must implore him to try again.* But before she could, Antuna spotted a sticky thread wrapped around a knot on the twig. *Thank the stars, Spifry is reeling us in.* Antuna slumped and rested as Spifry winched. The termite revived when they reached the shore, and Antuna half carried him to dry land.

"I see you like swimming and had to be the first one in the pool," Antuna joked. *I must lighten up this serious mood.*

"I've always hated water, and I'd be the last to jump into anything," coughed their new acquaintance as he rested. "I'm

Dinomite, and I am delighted to meet you. That was amazing. I owe you my life." Water dripped off his glossy, brass-colored head, revealing his long, sickle-like pincers. Six spindly legs extended from his coppery, accordion-shaped thorax, affixed to a slender, khaki-brown rippled abdomen.

Relieved that all were safe, Antuna justified her earlier desperation. "My parents drowned in a flood last hex. I couldn't save them, but I knew I could help you, Dinomite," she replied warmly. "That sort of thing is going around to-hexay." *And we're all working together.*

"Yeah, I resuscitated Antuna not so long ago." Antuna noticed Spifry stood tall as he spoke.

The words puzzled Dinomite, and he looked at Antuna intently. "You almost died too? But you were so strong!"

Antuna praised. "I couldn't have done it without Beegan and Beebie pushing so hard. And without little Spifry, I wouldn't even be here. He not only pulled us back to shore, but he also brought me back to life." *I'll never forget what he did.*

"Oh, I wasn't fishing for a compliment, only for ants and termites," joked Spifry, pretending to spit again at Antuna.

"I was only strong because Spifry filled me with his venom," chortled Antuna. "By the way, Spifry, it was great how you spat at the twig and didn't hit me." *You're the best in my book.*

"Yes, I just aimed at the knot," crowed Spifry, raising his forelegs to appear even taller.

"Thanks for that. It was outstanding." Antuna sprinkled a sparkly scent. "Welcome to our new world, Dinomite. I always wanted a termite friend." She stretched her antennae to reach Dinomite's.

"Well, you just got one," gushed Dinomite. "Thank you all."

Although Antuna was the youngest, she was the most

social and perhaps the most mature. Losing her parents and her displacement from her sisters cut her childhood short. Her stunted growth required her to move to another part of the hive, far away from them. She was a runt like Spifry, but matured quickly to fend for herself. Although her body size lagged, her personality surged, and her aunts and uncles described her as a tiny dynamo.

❦ ❦ ❦

After Dinomite and Antuna dried off, the new friends explored more. It invigorated Dinomite, having cheated death, and he moved with newfound determination. He hadn't been this animated since the day he metamorphosed from a larva to a nymph.

He perked up further when Antuna suggested further explorations. "If you're up to it, Dino, let's see what's at the edge where the new land starts."

"Yeah, I'm fine and curious too," agreed Dinomite. "I can check out my mound on the way." *This selfless heroine has completely shattered my glass-hard inclination to mistrust ants.*

"Okay, let's go around the far side of the marsh," proposed Beegan. "I see the new land starts over there."

"As long as we don't have to go into the water," joshed Dinomite, thrashing his limbs again.

Although joking, Dinomite's initial dislike of water became a genuine fear of water from that hexay forward.

"No, I'm done fishing for the hexay," kidded Spifry.

"Beegan and I can fly you over there to check it out," offered Beebie.

"No, let's walk," reasoned Dinomite. "We don't want to ruin the suspense."

They walked west for several hexutes and came across a

mound of freshly turned earth beneath another fallen bough from an old red oak.

"Hey, this is where my home termite mound was," mewled Dinomite, his voice dropping near a whisper. "The branch crushed it, and everything collapsed. I hope everyone's all right." *I must dig to save them.*

Dinomite cringed on hearing Antuna's report as she climbed to the other side of the bough. "I don't see any tunnels out," she called. "The branch might have squashed everyone!"

Two of the termites that had scrambled up the sinking branches approached Dinomite and told him what he did not want to hear. His face shifted, tormented by the news. *Don't tell me that!*

"What is it, Dino?" asked Antuna.

"My friends told me they saw the bough fall and the mound crumble," he moaned. "They tried to save those inside, but they only saved one." *I can't believe the limb killed all the others!*

"Was your family in there?" asked Beebie.

"All my relatives." Dinomite effused a flimsy fragrance and shook the earth off his back. *My efforts are futile.*

Spifry hopped onto the fallen limb. "Do you want us to help you dig?"

"No, it's too late," he cried. Then he pondered before stating, "Luckily, my parents said they'd be going out to the sequoia near the peach tree grove to-hexay. So, I should look for them." *I got to go right away.*

Beegan alighted from a short flight next to Spifry on the branch. "That's the way we're going."

～ ～ ～

Spifry tried his best to raise the spirits of his new friend Dinomite, but it didn't come easy for him. He never lost a family member or good friend because he'd never been close enough to anyone to call him buddy. Spiders were solitary creatures, never sure if another spider got close to them to be nice or to size them up for their next meal. So befriending Dinomite and the others was a first for him, and he found it refreshing to have post-pupae his age as companions, even from other species.

Spifry and his new acquaintances walked for several more hexutes until they were at the western edge of the marsh. The land from Earth had created a beach near an apple tree grove that preceded the peach trees.

"We're getting near my father's hunting grounds," reported Spifry. "He likes to catch wasps that feed on the apples from these trees." *Maybe I'll see him here.*

"Doesn't he get stung?" questioned Beebie, flashing her pointy spear.

"No, he spits at them and wraps them while they are stunned," Spifry explained, whipping his limbs to show a rapid victim spin. "He only bites them when they're exhausted from trying to get unwrapped." *We spiders are skilled at the kill.*

"Brilliant. Does your dad catch bees too?" asked Beebie, quivering.

Spifry giggled, observing Beebie quaking at spiders. *What would I do if she flew into my web?* His mother warned him about the deadly venom of bees and how he should stay as far away from them as possible. But these bees were not only non-threatening, but hospitable and even fearful of him.

"I don't think so," Spifry replied. "You guys are hard to wrap and too big to carry home. Although he sometimes brings the biggest wasps back to my mom as a gift." *I love my pa.*

"That's so sweet," gushed Antuna.

"Yeah, especially when they're covered with apple juice," laughed Spifry, wiping saliva from his dripping mandibles.

"Look over there at the beach. Is that a wasp's nest?" asked Dinomite, pointing at the shore with his pincers.

"Well, what's left of it," explained Beegan. "The fall broke the honeycombs, and the pulp is soaked."

"Are there any wasps in it?" enquired Antuna.

"No, they either flew away or drowned in the marsh," answered Beebie, flopping over to mimic a dead wasp.

Spifry laughed while watching Beebie. *I've never met a spider or insect that was so demonstrative.* His mother had taught him to hide his emotions, so Beebie's unbridled fervor captivated him, and he wasn't ashamed to show it. He followed Beebie's actions like a young ant imprinting on its colony-mates and, for a few hexutes, lost track of the discourse all around him.

"Looks like they drowned," added Dinomite. "I see many dead ones washed up on the beach."

"I see another nest too," exclaimed Beegan, hovering a little to get a better view.

"I bet many of them didn't survive this disaster," added Antuna. "Wasps often build their nests hanging from trees. The wasp I had earlier died when a gust knocked down his nest."

Beebie righted herself and shook off. "Their nests are so flimsy. I bet none of them survived."

Antuna motioned to the desolate landscape with her antennae. "Look, we're almost at the edge of the new land!"

Spifry snapped out of his momentary stupor and responded to Antuna. "It looks so barren. There are no plants," he said. "How could a spider even build a web?" *And what will I eat?* He looked at his new friends, who would typically be his lunch.

"Yeah, I only see rocks and dust," babbled Beebie, plunging

from her hover onto the ground. "It's like our neighborhood got picked up and dropped on the moon."

From their descriptions and accounts provided later, the planet they resettled was like Earth. Yet, it seemed to be in an era earlier than the Cretaceous period they left behind. The new world resembled Earth's Phanerozoic era before plants moved onto dry land. Volcanic rock and ash blanketed the land, and plant life had not yet emerged. The water holes throughout the planet were not marshes but Paleo-wetlands. The deep pools contained green and blue-green algae and large coral-like stromatolites essential for producing oxygen in the atmosphere. Although some blue-green algae are toxic to humans and insects alike, these algae appeared harmless to the new residents. None of these insects would ever order up algae on their plates, but they wouldn't turn down the oxygen it served them.

Our young explorers were on a slight stretch of their old land, with fruit trees and a narrow beach squeezed between the barren landscape on their left and the new marsh on the right.

Spifry noticed Dinomite straining to see what was on the beach ahead of them. "What are those silky sacks near the water?" he asked.

"That's probably my guys wrapping up wasps to take home to eat later," responded Spifry, tossing some silk over his back to display a dragging exercise.

Beebie stuttered out her next words. "Don't spiders only eat live meat?"

Spifry smiled at Beebie. "No, they'll take a dead insect as long as it's fresh." *I must teach her more about spiders, so she will not fear us.* "With this many wasps, they won't need to hunt again for hexths."

Spifry diverted his attention from Beebie back to Antuna.

Although amused by Beebie, Spifry was smitten with Antuna—or enamored like Beebie was with her sister Beegan. His heart swelled as he watched Antuna survey the landscape. Spifry couldn't deny that Antuna's charismatic confidence, which contrasted his own, instantly impressed him. He was often teased or ignored by other post-pupal spiders as a runt, so something inside him, he'd never understood until now, craved Antuna's 'sisterly' approval. Like Dinomite, Spifry adored Antuna.

"I see the spiders now," noted Antuna. "Is one of them your father?"

"I don't think so," replied Spifry. "My dad's web is a little to the east." And though he cared about his father, he was so thrilled to have new friends that he buried the worry for the moment. Instead, he grinned like a young spider taking flight on his first silk ballooning thread.

"But east of here is in there!" cried Dinomite, pointing to the marsh.

"What? Where are all the trees?" Spifry radiated a rocky reek. *The grove is only half the size I remember.* It seemed like his silk balloon flight landed in the middle of a forest fire, and dread overtook him.

Beegan soared over the marsh and came back with bad news. "I am sorry, Spifry. The marsh is deep, but I could see many apple trees still standing under the water. The marsh swamped everything east of here."

Spifry thought about all the fantastic times he had with his father when he was younger. *And he's been so great to my mom.* Then he realized his father might have survived. "My dad may be okay. He usually visits my mom in the mornings," he said, stamping his eight legs as he yearned to flee. "I'd better go now to see her. She lives up ahead in the peach tree grove."

"I'll go with you," stammered Dinomite. "That's near the sequoia tree I mentioned."

As Dinomite reached over to place an antenna on Spifry's back, he noticed Beegan turning back toward where they came. "Beebie and I should go home and check on our hive," she said.

"I'll go with you two." Antuna continued with little emotion. "Both my parents are dead, but my nest is near your hive."

"We could fly you there if you like," offered Beebie, showing her hooked claws.

"Yes, I'd like that," Antuna responded. Then she looked forlornly at Spifry and Dinomite. "Bye guys, I hope you both find your folks."

❦ ❦ ❦

As they flew back to the hive, Beebie spoke to Beegan with a soft scent, "I expect Dinomite is now an orphan and Spifry lost his dad."

"Maybe that's true, but they'll do like most insects," responded Beegan. "They'll forget their woe and move on."

Antuna, exhilarated by the flight, piped in a little late. "Yes, that's why we have such large families. So, we can care for each other when bad things happen. My uncles and aunts have raised me since I was little, and one of my older sisters even became the new queen."

As well as most of his termite community, Dinomite did indeed lose his parents. He learned they stayed in the mound to help extend a tunnel for some new eggs. Spifry also lost his father, who did not visit Spifry's mom that morning. But like Antuna, they put it behind them, and life went on. Perhaps finding new friends while grieving drew them closer to Antuna and the bee sisters. Even though these diverse insects and a spider would not customarily become friends, they pulled together. Antuna, her two bee girlfriends, Beegan and Beebie, and her rescuer and *rescuee*, Spifry and Dinomite, mostly remained friends for the rest of their lives. As they matured, they shared Antuna's altruistic and rebellious spirit. Given a second chance at life, Antuna would live it to the fullest. She never compromised her ideals, which were noble and unselfish. If there was a moral cause, Antuna was behind it for her entire long life, and her friends came along for the ride, although one of them strayed under pressure.

They were unsure whether it was the new atmosphere, the lack of cold winters, or reduced gravity and predation, but coming to the new planet extended all the new residents' life cycles. On Earth, the lifespans of this group of invertebrates ranged considerably, with a low of about a half-a-hexth for common houseflies up to six hexs for Formica ants. Here, they all lived about six times the natural life of an ant or one hexury. For these insects, the meteorite impact was the big bang in which their lives, as they knew it, changed forever. They had their own world, where they controlled their own destiny. It was liberating and daunting, but glorious. They loved the labor they lost without heavy lifting and their new tales devoid of winter.

CHAPTER 2

CAN'T WE WORK TOGETHER?

Colonies, like selves when young,
we need to shield and nurture.

And as they grow and inchmeal strive,
unveil their budding nature.

As they stretch and blossom,
they'll see their strength as awesome.

But to over-exercise one's stature may jeopardize all's future.

TWO OF THE most famous new arrivals on Poo-ponic were Beefirst and Genant. Beefirst was a queen bee, so the bees looked to her for leadership, and other insects feared her because of her great size. Being a queen bee, she was more the mothering type than a fighter, although she battled hard to save her subjects. Like most mothers, she cared for those under her guardianship, yet she was modest as a queen and uncorrupted by power. Beefirst took charge of nourishing the colony and making sure they had shelter. Times were hard until the plants and trees spread beyond the original Earth Island and provided more vegetation that these long-living insects needed to survive. Beefirst did her best to keep the Earth's plants healthy. She knew what to do to keep the colony whole. Although insects other than bees didn't appreciate it, her actions helped the colony.

Always humble, Beefirst reassured them, "I may hum if you ask me to sing, but if in need, come under my wing."

Beefirst was the Queen of Beegan and Beebie's hive, so they knew her well. They told Antuna and the guys how great she was. Beefirst's title intimidated Antuna, but she was still dying to meet her. She listened carefully when the bee sisters explained how Beefirst wanted to nourish their new world's plants and nurture a new cooperative spirit among the colony insects. Unlike most leaders that use fear and their followers' natural aggressive tendencies to sustain power, Beefirst inspired hope, understanding, and inclusiveness. It also delighted Antuna to learn that Beefirst was a creative leader, unconstrained by instinct, tradition, or customary practice.

Antuna stumbled upon the bee sisters by the marsh early one morning. "Beegan, I have to meet Beefirst. She is so fantastic." Her glance dropped from the sky to the ground. "I am unhappy with the leaders in my ant clan. All the female workers toil hard, and their sister soldiers will fight to the death for us. But they're all followers—none of them are role models." *I need inspiration from a leader who cares about others.*

"What about the male ants?" inquired Beebie. "Aren't they the managers?"

Unlike most ants currently on Earth, Formica ants in prehistoric times bred more drones than those needed for mating.

Although reproductive drones died after mating, the drones that did not mate lived long. Since they didn't have a defined social position in society, the non-maters freelanced at whatever role they believed would make them appear more powerful. Genant was an enormous ant that probably should have been a mating drone, but he elected not to mate so that he would live longer. His coppery skull was more rigid and twice the size of most other drones. In addition, his thoracic circumference was so bloated that it was difficult to tell where his extended abdomen began. This confusion was further complicated since both body segments appeared to have a blended brownish-black hue, which looked like a brass statue weathered for years.

Antuna shrugged. "Genant seems smart and strong, but he spends all his time planning to fight enemies, if we come across any. He is the general of the ants, and he fought to be commander of all the colony insects." She spread her forelimbs wide. "But I want to meet someone who cares about other insects and wants to bring us together in peace, not by force."

"Well, Beefirst is your girl," responded Beegan with utmost certainty. "She's all about everyone helping each other. What about the other drones?"

Antuna cleaned her antennae by sliding them through the setae hairs and brushes on her forelimbs. "I don't know. It seems like the guys have nothing important to do, and they spend their time studying or planning for war." *They're so awful to me and other females.* "They don't care about insects other than ants."

"Do you think they hate bees and beetles and other insects?" asked Beebie.

"Maybe not bees and beetles, but they don't like termites or spiders," answered Antuna, dribbling an abrasive aroma. "They don't fight for themselves, since our soldiers are all females.

Males are the supervisors and officers." *They love to order us all around.* "But don't get me droning on about them."

Beegan laughed lightly, "Good one, Tune. I'll try to get you an audience with the Queen."

"That'd be great!" cheered Antuna. *I'll count the hexays until I get that chance.*

"By the way, our parents told Beebie and me we'd be foragers." Beegan curled her front limbs as if she was gathering pollen. "Do you know what you're going to be when you grow up?"

Antuna felt a sense of dread wash over her. *I know the answer in my head, but I wish in my heart it was anything else.* "I haven't got my calling yet. My mother once told me I'd make a good soldier because I'm such a fighter. But I don't know if I can kill for a living." Antuna stretched her body and squirted a little formic acid to check her sprayer.

"I am sure you'll be great at whatever you do," Beegan stated delicately. Then not missing a beat, she said, "I never met another insect with more gumption than you."

"Gumption, that's a great word Sis, and fits Antuna like a worm's new skin," gushed Beebie.

"Thanks, girls," replied Antuna, requesting a three-way antennae tangle. "That means the world to me." *I couldn't have found better friends.*

Antuna felt she had regained the sisters she had lost many hexths before, and a warmth filled her. She admired Beegan for her wise and no-nonsense nature and appreciated Beebie's unbridled enthusiasm. The bee sisters, too, saw each of these characteristics in Antuna.

When the insects first arrived, it did not rain for several hexeks.

Many worried that the transplanted plants would not survive the drought, but as a creative thinker, Beefirst instructed the insects to collect all the plant seeds and sprouts they could and throw them into the murky edges of the large marsh near the colony. She also encouraged them to use the mire as a dump for their feces. Unlike the human equivalent, their insect excrement had antibacterial properties and made it a safe fertilizer. All the bees bought into the plan right away. But the other insects, especially the ants and termites, resisted at first. They did not want to listen to a bee, even if she was a queen.

When Beefirst heard that an influential young ant idolized her and wanted to meet her, she agreed right away to an audience. Beegan and Beebie brought Antuna to the hive to meet the Queen, leaving Antuna beside herself while being escorted into the hive. She had not had an audience with a queen since the day she moved across the nest, leaving her sisters and mother behind. Yet, she remembered many of the etiquettes her mother had taught her from when she was a nanitic. These included being diplomatic, caring for others, and exhibiting decisiveness when required.

Antuna marveled at the hive's magnificent structure, with honeycombs lining most walls and circular and hexagon-shaped tiles carpeting the floor. The honeycombs were color-coded in various yellow, orange, and brown shades, with clarity extending from water-like to dark molasses. The further they moved, the more she noticed the changing aromas of each, ranging from sweet raspberry to honeysuckle, nutty to spicy, or woody to earthy. Some smelled like aged cheese, and others like fresh-cut grass. Beegan explained that Beefirst liked to sort the varying flavors, which depended on the nectar source.

Antuna's awe continued when she first saw Beefirst. *She's*

twice the size of any bee I have ever seen! Her elongated abdomen dwarfed her long wings, and her yellow and black stripes were less defined, giving her body a coppery hue. She had less of a mane on her thorax than other bees, and the hairs on her fuzzy head sparkled with flecks of gold, in keeping with her royal status.

"Queen, your majesty, it's an honor to meet you." Outside, Antuna spouted a polished perfume, but inside she trembled. *I'm overwhelmed by excitement and anxiety about meeting such a powerful insect.*

"Oh, please, let's drop the formalities, my girl," replied Beefirst. "I may be a queen, but there's no need to curtsy or twirl. I'm dropping the rhyming right now because I want to talk with you seriously."

"Why? Am I in trouble?" murmured Antuna, the anxiety pushing through. "I hope I didn't offend you." *I've looked forward to this hexay for so long, and this was the last thing I wanted.*

Beefirst raised a wing over Antuna's shoulder. "On the contrary. Beegan and Beebie told me about you, and I need your help."

Antuna's antennae twitched more than when she absorbed Spifry's venom, then she asked hesitantly, "How could a young girl like me possibly help a queen?" *I didn't expect this.*

Beefirst looked Antuna over. "Your friends tell me you're a determined young ant. A girl with strong opinions and a sense of duty to her fellow insects. You're the one that was brought back to life by a spider, aren't you?"

"Yes, I owe Spifry my life," replied Antuna. "And I try to do my duty, but I'm still young, and my actions don't matter that much." Her antenna settled down.

"You've already done more than most of your leaders to

bring our insect families together," began Beefirst. "I hear you have close friends that are not only bees but also termites and spiders. Many insects have learned from your stories. They realize different insects can help each other out in these hard times, especially after the incident your friend Spifry called 'the displacement.' I like that word, but let's call it the Great Displacement," she proclaimed with a well-timed single flap of her massive wings.

"I am surprised our elders didn't forbid us from staying friends." *What would my parents say if they knew I'd befriended a spider and a termite?*

"On Earth, that would have happened," Beefirst explained. "But deep-down insects know that if we are going to survive here, we need to stick together. We must unite, at least until our little 'island from home' expands."

Antuna perked up at the Queen's comment. "You use *my* words now. I'm flattered, but how can I help you more?" *Now, this is a leader I can follow.*

Beefirst leaned closer to Antuna and whispered. "I can't force your leaders to accept my plans, and the more I push them, the more they resist. But if you and your friends can show them my plan is good, they may agree."

Antuna shrank a little. *Genant and the leaders hate young female ants like me.* "But how can I show them?"

Beefirst rubbed her claws together. "I need you and your friend Dinomite to pull off a little caper and some farming."

I must remain calm. Antuna hesitated. "Beg my pardon, Queen, but what do you mean?"

"You are getting formal again and rhyming, no less." Beefirst smiled.

Antuna giggled. "I didn't realize, but I still don't understand." Her laugh dissipated while she pondered the Queen's words.

"I've learned that both ants and termites store fungi in their burrows and feed on it when food is short," Beefirst explained. "And roaches live with ants because they love the fungi in ant nests."

"Yes, I know. I've had it many times," replied Antuna. "The roaches in our burrow would do anything for us if they could eat our fungi." *But I still don't know what you want.*

"In my flying hexays back on Earth," started Beefirst, flapping her wings a little to imitate flight. "I came across many marshes and swamps where fungi and algae grew together, helping each other out."

Antuna stood erect. *I must proclaim my ideas directly, as my mother taught me.* "Oh, wouldn't it be great if insect families could work together like that?"

"Girl, you are quick. That's exactly my goal."

"Where do I come in?" Antuna asked forthrightly. *I want to help.*

"No fungi grew on this planet when we arrived," Beefirst elaborated. "But I expect there still may be some fungi from Earth in ant and termite nests, or what's left of them."

"Yes, many of our burrows collapsed, but there are some fungi in those that didn't," responded Antuna. "I also know where the collapsed nests are, and we could excavate them."

Beefirst grinned and gushed a bright bouquet. "Beegan told me you were quick."

"You want me and Dinomite to raid our nests for fungi or dig it out of the old burrows and bring it to the marsh?" *I must show her I'm on top of this.*

"Exactly, but there's more. We also need poo, lots of poo,"

explained Beefirst. "Fungi grow well in nests because they thrive on dung."

"Well, that'll be fun! My friend Spifry can spin his thread into bins to help us carry it from the burrows." *I'm sure she'll love this.* "I'll tell everyone it's a science project we're doing."

"Girl, you make my stinger seem dull." Beefirst laughed richly. "It seems you know what to do. When the others see your experiment working so well, they will follow," she proclaimed, then stood tall and flapped her wings to show the audience was over.

Antuna left her meeting with Beefirst more impressed with the Queen than before and more confident than she had been in a long time. She cherished knowing that the zeal she possessed not only impressed the Queen but had a purpose that matched her lofty ideals.

❧ ❧ ❧

As Beefirst predicted, Antuna and Dinomite's science experiment worked like a charm. And the Queen's plan performed brilliantly. The algae and the poo helped the fungi flourish in the marsh. Antuna and Dinomite gave out samples to all the colony insects. Everyone enjoyed the fungi, some of which tasted like chocolatey, nutty truffles, while others resembled garlicky portobello mushrooms. So, they immediately embraced Beefirst's plan. Most colony insects brought fungi spores, seeds, and sprouts to the marsh's edge, and everyone defecated there daily. Beefirst's strategy became a lifesaver—although the outer edges of the marsh dried a little, fungi and young plants thrived in a well-fertilized oasis-like shoreline. Antuna's new fungi farm sustained the colony until the rains returned. Even though these fungi flourished, other fungi that live off dying plants did not survive. This loss slowed the progress of vegetative growth. The spread of plant life hinged instead on insect activity for turning over and producing soil from decaying plants and trees. Indeed, one could say they toiled and troubled till their soil was overturned and many times doubled.

Beebie's soupy marsh and Antuna's fungi farm were the focal points of life-supporting nutrients in the most desperate times. So grateful for its contribution to the colony's early survival, the insects named the planet after Beefirst's vital hydroponic system. They called it Poo-ponic. Insects use their feces for many things, including shelter construction, attracting mates, and fertilizing plants. They even used it for deterring enemies back on Earth, though they never flung their dung.

As life remained challenging in the first hexs after they arrived on the planet, Beefirst encouraged the colony insects to work together. Many insects learned from Antuna's example, and various species joined forces. After the success of the science experiment, Antuna planned to give a presentation to the entire colony to encourage further interspecies cooperation. She convinced her friends to interview various leaders about how diverse insect families were helping each other out.

Antuna volunteered to do the first consultations. "I'll interview the top ants and termites in my burrow. Can you guys quiz some of the other families?" *I'm sure it'll be fun.*

Beegan flapped her wings to signal her pride as a flying insect. "Beebie and I will question Beefirst and the leader of the flies."

Dinomite snapped his pincers. "Okay, I'll handle the termites and beetles."

Spifry lowered himself close to the ground. "Guess that leaves me the spiders and worms."

Antuna left that afternoon to start her interviews, but she had difficulty finding an ant that would talk to her. They didn't seem so happy with a young ant playing with other insects, leaving her initial confidence waning. Thankfully, Genant's second in command, Major Assistant, who loved tasty fungi, agreed to see her.

"You're the one that did the science experiment and discovered those wonderful varieties of fungi, aren't you?" asked Assistant.

Antuna cautiously approached him. "Yes, you liked them?" *Maybe this guy will help.*

"Oh yes," responded Assistant. "It's the best stuff I ever tasted. How did you ever figure out that algae would enhance the fungi?" he continued as excessive saliva dripped from his enormous jaws.

"I'll be happy to tell you if you can answer a few questions for me," responded Antuna. *I think he will assist.*

Assistant reached out to pat Antuna on the shoulder. "Yes, of course. What do you want to know?"

Antuna looked down at her notes quickly. "Could you tell me the ways ants are helping the community?"

"The ant community?" asked Assistant.

Antuna spread her forelimbs wide. "No, the whole insect society." *Uh oh, I might be wrong about him.*

Assistant put a claw to his temple, "Oh gosh, I'll have to think about that—ah, we dump our poo in the marsh and harvest all the fungi we can, and the roaches eat it too."

"Is that all?" queried Antuna. *Shouldn't I get more from*

Genant's second in command? But, yet once again, her interaction with a drone dropped like a stone.

"Yes, but let me give you a nice rhyme that you can quote me on," bragged Assistant.

"Yes, do you need some time?" asked Antuna. *Okay, he's helping.*

Assistant looked out the door, seeping a soggy smell. "Uh-huh."

After a full five hexutes, Assistant gave her a quote for the article, rearing up for emphasis. "Ants are happy to donate our poo to provide fungi for all of you."

Almost too embarrassed to use the quote, Antuna hid it well down in the pheromonal report she prepared on the exercise.

Undaunted, Antuna sought a high-ranking roach for their survey. She was happy when the Topshell of the cockroaches, Roachester, agreed to take part. In a lengthy interview, Antuna got Roachester to explain the symbiotic relationship between ants and roaches.

"Although ants attack some types of roaches, our group produces pheromones that make us smell like the ants," Roachester rolled over and released a puff of his pleasant scent.

"Is that because you want ants to love you?" *It's funny how it's so much easier for me to talk to a roach than a male ant.*

"Well, sort of, but we want ants to treat us as if we were their own," replied Roachester.

Antuna sampled the air to pick up Roachester's scent. "Why is that so important?"

Roachester's salivary glands swelled. "Well, it's selfish, I guess. But we love the fungi generated in ants' nests."

Antuna shrugged. "But fungi are now available at the marsh." *I guess you don't need us anymore.*

Roachester spun around, seemingly unsure of what to say. "Yes, but we've done this for so long, and where else would we live?"

"What's in it for the ants?" queried Antuna. *Our guys give nothing away for free.*

Roachester rose into a menacing stilt-stance and explained, "We protect ant eggs and young, but we like to protect everyone in the colony who needs our help."

Antuna pulled some chalk from her pouch. "Can you sum it up in a good quote for our report?"

Roachester remained in his elevated posture. "Sure, I've got a line that explains the ant-roach dynamic well: 'Our musk is not meant to deceive. It is part of the trust we weave.'"

Antuna supplemented the report with some facts she researched about the colony protections Genant had developed since taking over as colony commander.

※　※　※

Beebie urged Beegan to start on the project right away. Like Antuna, she idolized Queen Beefirst and hoped she could make a good impression while interviewing her. She knew that Beegan usually dominated in these circumstances, but she wanted to take charge for once. The sisters set out the same afternoon for their interviews, and as they expected, it pleased the Queen to oblige.

Beebie first asked the Queen, "What are you doing to help other insect families?" *I hope she recognizes my initiative.*

"As Queen, I have provided honey to insects in need." Beefirst pointed her antennae towards her vast honeycomb.

"Wow, that's amazing," Beebie responded, flapping her wings rapidly. *That's so generous, and I bet she's trying to encourage cooperation.* "Are the other bees supportive?"

Beefirst shuffled over toward the nearest honeycomb to

assess its condition. "Yes, I've polled our top workers and soldiers, who agreed that we'll share our honey with anyone who wants it when times are tough. Bees are very giving and particularly caring for the needy."

Beebie quizzed the Queen further, "Is this program already in place?" *See, I can be as probing as Beegan.*

Beefirst looked out the entrance to the hive and secreted a smooth scent. "Yes, these are hard times after the Great Displacement, so the honey is on us."

"Guess that puts you in a sticky position, so to speak." Beebie chortled and licked her claws. *My humor should win her over.*

Beefirst broke into a wide grin. "Right you are, Beebie, but the flies have agreed to help transport nectar, which will double our production."

"Thank you, Queen," interjected Beegan. "Can you give us a quote for our report?"

"Of course, here's one: 'If you have little else to eat, you'll find our honey is quite the treat.'" Beefirst reached toward the honeycomb and offered Beebie and Beegan a couple of dollops.

Beebie leaned over to Beegan as they left the hive. "Thanks for letting me do most of the asking, Sis."

"No problem, I could tell you wanted to make an impression," replied Beegan.

The bee sisters continued with their interviews the following morning. Once again, they scored big with one of the top flies in the colony, Flyhi.

Beebie again started the questioning, "What efforts are flies making to help other insects?" *I'm not keen to impress this time, but I'm on a sweet roll.*

"Well, as everyone knows, flies are good citizens and lend a claw or a wing whenever asked," replied Flyhi. "We're struggling a little right now after the upheaval, but we agreed to help the bees collect nectar to increase honey production." Flyhi made a sucking motion to show how flies collect nectar.

"Anything else?" asked Beegan. *These guys are helpful. I've always liked flies.*

Flyhi looked around to see if anyone else was listening. "Last hexek, Genant asked if we would perform reconnaissance flights to observe the settlers' movements to ensure their safety, and we agreed."

"Okay, that's great," responded Beegan, catching his wee whiff. "Can we quote you in our report?"

Flyhi pondered briefly. "Yes, here's something I said to Beefirst recently: 'Getting our jaws round this nectar stuff is tricky, but when cooked, there's no better way to get sticky.'"

Flyhi confirmed Beebie's optimistic expectations about flies. They bought into Beefirst's goal of insect-wide collaboration, and they were law-abiding colonists that put society before themselves.

⁂

Dinomite didn't start his interviews until the following hexay, thinking the exercise was a good idea but concerned about the reactions he might get. Although he approached many termites, only one of them agreed to talk, and Dinomite accurately perceived it was not because his subject supported the cause. So Dinomite approached Captain Slimite, the third-ranking termite officer, carefully.

Slimite looked Dinomite over, shooting a sharp stink. "You're that kid who plays with ants and bees. No wonder no termite will talk to you."

Dinomite pushed on, "But didn't termites cooperate with

the ants and Beefirst in the fungi farming project?" *I can't believe it. What a jerk. Like all the others.*

Slimite groomed his pincers. "I don't want you to quote me on this, but I'll answer. Termites had already planned an algae-fungi experiment when you and that ant-girl pulled your little stunt." He sneered at Dinomite. "Of course, we added our poo to the project, as we planned to do it, anyway. But we extracted the fungi our poo fertilized so no one else could steal it."

Dinomite felt Slimite only agreed to talk to him, to smarten him up. *I don't think termites are into cooperation.*

Slimite wanted him to realize that the rank-and-file termites reviled the colony's new direction and resisted Beefirst's inter-play between insect families, especially if it included ants.

Dinomite did not have any better luck landing an interview with a top beetle because the beetles did not have any genuine leaders. After going from tree to tree, he finally found a well-known beetle named Beetlebob.

"So, Beetlebob, what are beetles doing to help other colony insects?" asked Dinomite. *I hope this interview goes better.*

"We wood-boring beetles help any insect taking a walk or fly about," replied Beetlebob, emitting a balmy bouquet. "We bore holes in trees, and when it's wet or too hot, you can come and hole up in our bores." He wriggled a little to show how to enter a borehole. "If you want to, you can stay there for hexays."

Dinomite scribbled down some notes. "Anything else?" *At least beetles don't care who I play with.*

"I know the queen bee," Beetlebob replied. "What's her name, Beeworst? She tells her bees to take sap from our boreholes when they can't find any nectar. That's okay. There's more than enough to go around. The sap's also tasty and gives you energy for long journeys." He looked over both shoulders. "And I'm a teetotaler, but when the sap leaks down and pools on a rock, it'll ferment. I'm told it makes a nice brew." Beetlebob turned toward his stash. "I'll get you some I collected last hexek, and you can take it home for you and your friends to try."

Dinomite tossed his chalk from one claw to the other, buoyed by his subject's comments. "Great, can you give me a quote for our report?" *I got some excellent stuff here.*

Beetlebob popped his head back out of the borehole as he entered. "What, didn't I give you enough already?"

Dinomite's heart skipped a beat, then he calmed himself and quipped, "Just a rhyme for our story."

Beetlebob snickered. "Oh, okay. A large group of bees and flies got rowdy after finding a nice brew of strong sap. I saw them staggering around as they were getting ready to fly back to the colony. I called out to them, 'It looks like you flying bunch have been into the strong sap. Before you go, come into my boreholes and take a long nap.' I thought that was good advice."

Dinomite didn't know any beetles, so he didn't know what to expect before the interview. Yet, he felt he came away with an accurate impression of their general attitude. Although not a leader of the beetles, Beetlebob's demeanor reflected the feelings of most beetles. Dinomite concluded they were a modest group that stuck to themselves, but were delighted to share what they had with other insects. They mostly lived and worked in healthy trees, and they didn't find termites, ants, or roaches threatening, as these other groups usually foraged within fallen timbers.

❦ ❦ ❦

Spifry waited for almost a hexek before starting his interviews. He had drawn the short end of the stick, probing inter-insect cooperation with the only two non-insect species on the planet.

He expected the lead spiders weren't interested and might even be nasty to him, so the more he procrastinated, the longer he could prolong the inevitable. In the end, Spifry questioned his mother, Spima. She was the second-ranked spider soldier and a perfect candidate in his eyes. He resolved to reveal that the subject of the interview would remain anonymous.

His interview was terse, and he only asked two questions. "Mom, what are spiders doing to help colony insects?" *If anyone knows, my mum does.*

Spima approached Spifry and dusted off his coat with a maternal gentleness. "Well, my little Spifry, I could poll my colleagues, but there's no need. I know what they're thinking."

Spifry recoiled. *I wish she'd stop treating me like a larva.* "What's that, Ma?"

"We'll do whatever we can to help fatten you guys up." Spifry's mother smiled knowingly, with saliva dripping from her maws. A frosty fragrance chilled the air.

Spifry recognized that his mother's sentiment foreshadowed a problem that had not yet surfaced. There had been no insect captures since the spiders were still living off the corpses that they collected their first few hexays on the new planet. The future scenario was a quandary for which even Beefirst had no solution—spiders eat meat. Spifry knew spiders could be friendly, but their desires and instincts became primary when they were hungry.

Spifry's second interview went much better. But like Dinomite's questioning of the beetles, the worms didn't have a leader, so he quizzed the only one he knew.

"So Wormwurst, can you tell me how worms help other colony insects?" enquired Spifry. *I know worms can be quite helpful.*

"Sure, honey, we dig most tunnels around here,"

Wormwurst started, seeping a snug scent. "We dig out burrows and the beehive shafts, and we move stones. We may be shy, but we like to help, and no one can say we don't pull our weight around here."

Pushing around the soil is so dirty. I'm glad the worms are doing it. "Can you give me a quote for our story?"

"Sure, sweetie, you can see that I'm a full-figured gal." Wormwurst contracted her longitudinal muscles to expand her circumference to the maximum. "So, when they wanted some extra wide channels for the beehives, they asked for me. I was so happy to oblige. It's nice to know this bod is good for something. You can quote what I said to the head honey-comber: 'Great to know my wide girth has some proper use and worth. Better keep me from the honey, else change my name to Two-tunny.'"

Spifry laughed but then thought seriously about how worms contributed to the colony. *Like us spiders, they're not insects. But at least worms do not eat insects, and they are quiet supporters.* Indeed, they never refused when asked for help and took intense pride in their work. Beefirst recognized these qualities when she looked for members in her new multi-species partnership.

⁂

Antuna presented their report to anyone interested in an 'open-burrow' at the main square next to the marsh. It was a small assembly, with mostly bees, flies, beetles, and worms in attendance. Though she felt a pinch of nerves initially, everyone who saw it said she did a fantastic job, easing any building anxiety. After the presentation, Antuna and her young friends went back to her nest to celebrate. Dinomite brought the strong sap from Beetlebob, and they sampled it and found it delightful, like maple syrup-sweetened spruce beer.

"Thank you, Dinomite. This helped calm my nerves," said Antuna with breathless relief.

Embarrassed by their subpar contributions, Dinomite and Spifry found it cheered them up. The bee sisters were in the mood for a party, drank their share, and got tipsy. They had a good time, and nobody overdid it, but they each had an unrelenting headache in the morning. As for the rest of the settlers, the tough times pulled the friendly insects together, and they cultivated ties between their families that strengthened the community. But as shown by the group's survey, some bonds were more robust than others.

❀ ❀ ❀

As time passed, the colony took shape. With its fungi farm shores north of the burrows, the marsh became the focal point of the community. Antuna, her ant colony, and their roach nest-mates lived right at the center of the marsh shoreline, next to the main central beehive. Honeybees rarely built their hives below ground, but Beefirst constructed the hive underground for safety. She had seen other bees do this on Earth and did not see any reason honeybees couldn't. She also wanted the new colony to cooperate and enlisted the worms to excavate their underground hive since honeybees didn't dig.

One hexay, Antuna found Beegan sunning herself just outside their beehive, wet and shivering.

"Hi Antuna, I got wet in the rain this morning, and it takes forever to dry my fuzzy coat," complained Beegan with a stutter.

Antuna wriggled a little, as if burrowing. "Beegan, do you

find it odd having to go underground to get into your new hive?" *If I were you, I'd worry about my wings getting dirty.*

"It's a little strange," replied Beegan, but then gave it some more thought. "But after what happened to the wasps, I feel safer underground."

Beebie came out of the hive just in time to hear the question. "Beefirst said the honey would be safer there, too. But who would want to steal it?"

"At least she got the worms to dig out the tunnels," Beegan said. "It's not something I wanted to do. It was bad enough when I got buried when we first arrived here."

"I'm glad they dug the hive next to our burrow." Antuna exuded a sweet smell. "It's like we're next-door neighbors." *I love having my new BBFs (best bee friends) so close. We're inseparable.*

"Yes, and of course, Genant insisted on having the ant and roach nest right at the center of the marsh," scoffed Beebie.

"Well, you know Genant, he always gets his way," admitted Antuna. *I am embarrassed as an ant.*

Beegan pointed to the east. "And you have that lovely jungle with the palm trees on the other side."

"Yeah, it's where the flies sleep at night," replied Antuna. *I can't believe they're outside all night.*

Antuna knew the flies congregated in the palm trees on the other side of the ant-roach burrows because they preferred not to live underground. Instead, Flyhi and his mates often slept on the underside of leaves in the adjacent palm tree grove. Fan palms have many long leaves that let the flies cluster together to shield themselves from the rain. They also liked the stand of palms on the east side of the ant-roach nests. Flyhi encouraged many flies to feed and lay their eggs there on a rather rank side of the marsh, where the fungi smelled more. Antuna supposed these fungi took up the blue-green algae, which were more prevalent on that side of the marsh. The fungi reeked like the rotting flesh of animals and fruit, their regular diet. The fungi also had proteins that the flies and their larvae needed to survive. Their fungi diet was vital, since they could no longer find animal dung or rotting carcasses. Their fungi may have smelled, but it kept their tummies swelled.

"The worms are our neighbors on the other side," continued Beegan. "It's good to have them close when they dig the tunnels for us."

Antuna moved close to the bees and whispered, excreting a delicate fragrance, "I heard they chose the west side, since they wanted to be far from the flies." *I wonder if they know the story.*

Beebie trembled a little, and the more Antuna studied her movements, the more she saw her empathy for worms. "Yes, Wormwurst told me they're afraid of flies," she said.

"Back on Earth, they had a terrible experience with a family of cluster flies whose larvae killed some of them," explained Antuna. *I'm sure this will shock Beebie.*

"What do you mean?" asked Beebie, trickling a pulsating vapor.

"The fly larvae dug their way through the soil and attached themselves to the worms," Antuna explained with her jaws snapping. "Then they entered them and ate them from the inside out." *I think she'll freak.*

Beebie froze with disbelief. "No wonder they fear them."

"Yes, I heard about that, but only cluster flies do it," assured Beegan. "Housefly larvae don't eat earthworms. So, the worms shouldn't fear them."

"But houseflies look like cluster flies," noted Beebie, and then she shook again.

Beebie's terrified. I better change the subject. "Hey, why do we call them houseflies when they sleep outdoors?"

"On Earth, they ate animal dung and carcasses," explained Beegan, who prided herself on her excellent knowledge of fly foraging. "So, they would go into the animals' dens, lairs, and nests to raid their stuff."

"And now they eat the stinky fungi near the jungle." Beebie retracted her antennae to block the scent detectors.

"Did you hear that Dinomite and the other termites from his mound joined another family with a nest next to the worms?" gossiped Beegan.

"Yes, they're at the western end of the colony, near where his mound collapsed," responded Antuna. *Poor Dinomite, I can't imagine how hard it must have been.*

Beegan pointed down. "But they built underground instead of creating above-ground mounds this time."

"Smart," Beebie considered.

Beegan added, "I heard the worms offered to dig for them, but they said no."

Antuna raised her shoulders and let out a scoff. "Yeah, they said they already knew how to dig. It's like building mounds, but upside down." *At least they learned from it, I think.*

Ever perceptive, Antuna determined that termites did not need help, but they also did not want worms around. Despite Beefirst's early befriending of the worms, various insect families harbored a deep wariness of worms, as they did not have legs and were not insects. However, the worms did not disturb the others and were not aggressive.

"And is Dinomite happy there?" asked Beebie.

"No, he's having a hard time fitting in," Antuna groaned. *I wish I could help him.* "The new termite teens are very cliquey."

"That's too bad," Beegan said. "And what about Spifry and the other spiders?"

"They have spread all around, in various trees and bushes," Antuna replied. *I'm glad she changed the subject.*

As Antuna well knew, Spifry and his spider mates, like flies, did not like to live underground. They lived in trees and bushes dotted throughout the colony, avoiding the marsh shoreline as they eschewed fungi. Many assembled in the grove of apple trees beyond the marsh's edge in an area northwest of the termite burrow. Spifry explained to Antuna that spiders lived on their webs, which needed to be up on trees or bushes where flying insects flew.

The spiders did not struggle in the early hexays because they fed off many insects killed during the Great Displacement. As our young insects discovered on their walk-about, spiders had the foresight to gather up many of the carcasses that littered the countryside that first hexay—wrapping them up kept them for a while. After they gathered large amounts, the spiders went for a long time without hunting. They savored their meal for some time, first liquifying it, then sucking the fluid into their foregut for storage before transporting it to their hindgut. Only when their hindguts were empty did they get the urge to eat again; as the spiders would always say—*waist knot, want not.*

"I hope Spifry got some food, like the spiders on the beach," said Beegan.

"Yes, even though he was sad about his dad, his mom forced him to gather some carcasses." Antuna rubbed her tummy. "He had quite an enormous belly the last time I saw him."

"With so many dead wasps and other insects, most spiders have swollen bellies," said Beebie, puffing herself up.

"Yes, and I guess that's why Genant hasn't forced them out

of the colony," stated Beegan. "I haven't heard of any spider attacks or anyone getting caught on a web yet."

Beegan suggested they move a little to the west, with the solar star shifting so that they were now in the shade. "It'll just be another few hexutes. I'm almost dry."

Looking up at the tree casting the shadow, Beebie continued to ask about the new planet's residents. "And what about the beetles? Where did they go?"

"Oh, they're around, but they don't like fungi," replied Antuna. "They're mostly in the forest behind the burrows." *I don't know any beetles, but I know they work hard and get things done.*

Beetlebob and the wood-boring beetles lived in a large grove of sequoia trees that bordered the south side of the colony farthest from the marsh. This grove extended south of the central beehive and southeast behind the ant and roach nests. The beetles usually only bored into the bark. But if the tree was an old, weak one, the beetles would bore right through it in time, taking the giant tree down.

Beebie continued, "I don't know that many beetles. They keep to themselves."

"Well, we can thank them for the lovely strong sap," added Beegan with a pleasing disposition. "It only ferments after leaking from the beetles' boreholes."

"Yeah, we should get Dinomite to visit Beetlebob and get some more," chuckled Antuna. *If only we could stay friends like this forever.*

Aside from their role in strong sap production, the beetles also helped spread sequoia seeds. They laid their larva in sequoia pine cones, where the young ones ate the flesh of the cone scale, causing it to erupt and the seeds to disperse. Beetlebob often bragged how his emergence from the pinecone showered the forest floor with seeds to celebrate the pupae coming into the world. Most often boring only bark and helping the forest by dispersing seeds and felling old dying trees, these beetles aided in keeping the forest healthy. Many beetles, like Beetlebob, lived in this grove but would venture out to find dying sequoias to take down, establishing outposts throughout the area.

Although the Earth Island included a landmass that extended about three-square miles, the damage done to many nests and hives forced many insects to move or rebuild. When the insects saw the successful fungi farms at the marsh, every-one wanted to live nearby. The marsh colony was the place to be, and insects from the entire Earth Island migrated there. Beefirst and the other leaders were happy to welcome them. The more poo, the better the fungi farm. The insects of each family expanded their burrows to accommodate everyone. Antuna recognized the general feeling: *we can't refuse when you bring your refuse.*

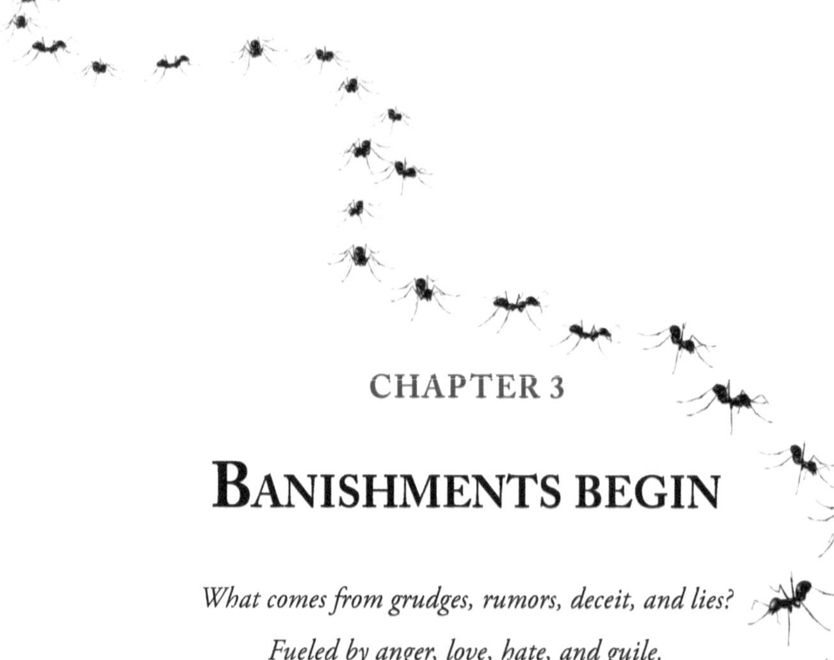

CHAPTER 3

BANISHMENTS BEGIN

What comes from grudges, rumors, deceit, and lies?
Fueled by anger, love, hate, and guile.
That which robs our selfless tries and
transplants fight in place of smile.

AFTER HEXS PASSED by, the now teenage friends thought about what the future had in store and questioned what they would do when they grew up. Then they received some disturbing news that crushed their rosy dreams. The termite elders prohibited Dinomite from congregating with members of other insect families, leaving Antuna distraught.

"This is against everything we have fought for," cried Antuna, thrusting her forelimbs up in frustration. "And they ripped poor Dinomite from his friends."

"You know Dinomite is a little older than us," responded Spifry, trying to find some reason in the order. "I expect they are grooming him to join the army. Their armies almost always fight ants, and they want to make sure he knows whose side he's on." *I wish I could console her.*

"That is so unfair!" complained Antuna. "Why do we always have to fight each other? We're on a new planet here. Can't we do things differently?"

"Yeah, I get strange looks from my family," Spifry said solemnly. "And I know what they're thinking. 'Why are you playing with those girls when you should eat them?'" *Oops, I shouldn't have said that.*

Antuna's brow puckered. "You wouldn't do that, would you, Spifry?"

Spifry fixed his gaze on her. *I can't believe she asked me that. Haven't I proved to her my feelings?* But then, realizing her question was more out of paranoia than fear, he was determined to reassure her. "I would never even dream of attacking you, Dinomite, or the bee sisters."

Antuna gave him a slight smile.

"But spiders need to eat meat," Spifry continued. *She must know it's difficult for me.* "And I've been consuming lots of seeds and pollen lately. I like the shore fungi too, but my mother says I should avoid it because the spores can make us sick."

Just then, Beegan and Beebie flew in with some urgent news.

"Antuna, I got a message from a friend of Dinomite," Beegan voiced with a pale perfume. "He says Dinomite wants to meet us, but it has to be a secret."

Beebie nodded. "He wants us to come to the hollowed-out log by the apple tree where the beehive used to be. Do you know the place?"

Antuna thought for a hexond and smiled. "Yes, my dad used to take me there to sample aphid honeydew, but I have seen no aphids since the Great Displacement."

"It's close to the old sagebrush with my web," said Spifry, crawling closer to Antuna. "Where I first saw Antuna carrying the dead wasp." *Just before we all became friends.*

"When did he want to meet?" queried Antuna.

"Tonight, after the setting of the solar star," replied Beebie.

"It's already past noon!" stammered Spifry, twitching his eight legs. "We'll have to leave right now if we want to make it in time." *She better not suggest we fly.*

Beegan flapped her wings rapidly. "Don't worry," she exclaimed. "Beebie and I can carry each of you. Flying will be much faster."

"Yes, I enjoyed our last flight," bubbled Antuna.

Spifry wafted a vacillating vapor and backed away from the group. "Well, okay, but you'll fly low, I hope." *But I think walking would be better?*

"Yeah, no worries, Spi," Beebie buzzed. "We'll get you there safely."

Beegan smiled in agreement. "We'll come to pick you up in two hexours."

❧ ❧ ❧

Meanwhile, over at the termite barracks, Dinomite was enduring a lecture from his new superior. Although he made some rookie mistakes, Dinomite was enthusiastic about his new position. He saw the army as his new purpose and a way to replace the termite relationships he lost when his mound collapsed.

"You'll have to shape up, soldier, and leave your childish ways behind you," commanded Sargemite.

Dinomite stood at attention. "Yes, of course, Sargemite." *Does he think I'm still a nymph?*

Sargemite sprayed a solid stink. "That's, *Yes, sir,* Private."

"Yes, sir." Dinomite stood as straight as possible. *Okay, okay. I hate all these rules.*

"And you have to lose your looney friends," ordered Sargemite. "We don't want you fraternizing with the enemy."

"They're not..." *Ah, I can't say that.* "Yes, sir."

"That's right, private, and get used to saying, *yes, ma'am,* when you come across our female officers," growled Sargemite.

"Yes, ma'am?" Dinomite stammered, eager to get away. "Er, yes, sir!"

※ ※ ※

Later, Beegan and Beebie returned to collect Antuna and Spifry. Antuna was bouncing with excitement, but Spifry looked a little green. He came by a fear of flying instinctively, as birds were key predators of spiders back on Earth. So, in his mind, if you were flying, you were probably some bird's dinner or fodder for their young.

"Okay, flyers, are you ready?" enquired Beegan.

"Yep, already got my wings on," giggled Antuna, flapping her middle limbs.

Spifry backed away and stooped low. "Guess so." *If I must, I must.*

"Well, climb aboard," crowed Beebie again, flapping her wings.

Spifry shuttered and closed his eyes as Beegan grabbed him with her claws.

And with that, they took off to the west and towards the setting solar star. The four friends spoke little as they covered the distance. Antuna enjoyed every hexond, while Spifry closed his eyes and couldn't wait until they landed. Antuna asked if they could go any faster, and Spifry insisted they fly lower. As the hexay-light waned and the bees sped up and flew lower, Beebie and Antuna flew right into a spider web. The web's owner was a larger-than-large female spider who hadn't fed for hexays.

"Oh no, Beebie's hit a web!" Beegan discharged a screeching stink. "That monster of a spider is after them."

Spifry opened his eyes wider than he ever had before and declared, "I know that spider. Spifrida, she's a nasty one." *I could never take her on. She'll have me for dinner.*

Spifrida approached Antuna, who was closest, and acrid-smelling saliva spewed beneath her fangs. "What do we have here? Honeybee with a side of ant."

Spifry fretted at the thought of losing Antuna and Beebie to a spider, one of his kind. Yet he knew he couldn't reason with a slobbering spider zeroing in on her prey. *What can I do? What should I do?*

Spifrida bore down on Antuna, who froze in shock and the sticky spirals when Beebie freed herself, jumped between them, and exposed her stinger. "Any closer, and you'll taste *my* venom!"

For a moment, Spifry marveled at Beebie's bravery. *I guess she'll back off at the sight of that.* Relief flooded through him at the thought that he might not have to act.

Spifrida slowed her progress at first, but in the blink of an eye, she spat at Beebie and knocked her back on her wings, stunning her. Then she sidled close and wrapped Beebie up in silk.

Beegan flew as fast as she could through the web's bridge thread on one side. The mainline snapped, and the whole web flipped end over end, with Beebie dropping to the ground below. The web doubled over Antuna, who became more entangled than ever, as Spifrida catapulted casually over to the opposite ring of spirals.

Spifrida surmised, "Guess my side has become my main."

Spifry, who had jumped off Beegan onto the opposite auxiliary spiral, bellowed at Spifrida, "Don't touch her, you brute, or I'll...." *I can't let her get Antuna!*

Spifrida interrupted him, standing upright on her hind legs. "Oh! You hungry yourself, Smallfry? You have some *latro* threatening me. What are you going to do?" she smirked.

"I'll knock you on your spinnerets, you mother," yelled Spifry. *You can't string up my friend.*

"Smallfry, I heard your spit is so pathetic you couldn't take down an aphid," mocked Spifrida.

Antuna snapped out of her stupor, unstuck herself, and charged down the spirals toward Spifrida.

Beebie, who struggled to unwrap herself below the web, shrieked louder than an entire orchestra of crickets at dusk, "Nooo!!"

Spifry spewed a sizzling stench. *She won't notice me with all this commotion.* He completely emptied his venom sack on a wad of spitting thread he had been generating since they arrived.

"It's Spifry, you witch!" he yowled, releasing a spit that hit Spifrida right between the eyes, knocking her off the web.

Spifrida convulsed a little while, stunned and frozen on the ground next to Beebie. Spifry smiled and stood tall, beaming with newfound pride. *I showed you!*

Beebie, now completely unwrapped, yelled, "Let's get out of here," and she smashed through the tattered web and grabbed Antuna.

"Yes, ma'am." Beegan immediately swooped over and snatched Spifry.

As they flew off together, Antuna looked over at Spifry, who, with eyes wide open, had crawled up on Beegan's back and stood as tall as he could. "Looks like you gave a whole new meaning to the word fry, Spi."

Spifry looked back and beamed. *I may be small, but you can count on me.* Then, when they arrived at the hollowed-out log, he leaned over to Antuna and said, "Whatever were you thinking rushing at Spifrida like that? She'd have skewered you in a hexond."

Antuna smiled in response. "I wanted to distract her, and I knew you had great aim. From now on, I'm calling you Fry, and not because you're small."

Spifry swelled with pride, cherishing his growing connection with Antuna. He'd gone from having no friends to some of the best he could have imagined. *No one is going to take my friend away from me.*

※ ※ ※

When the party arrived at the meeting site, Dinomite emerged from the hollowed-out log and uttered, "Friends, I am so happy that you could come. I wasn't even sure if you got the message." *I am excited to see my friends. But will this be the last time?*

"Of course, we came," Antuna professed. "We'd cross marshes or hot coals to see you."

Dinomite stamped his limbs, then chuckled. "Hot coals! Have you been lighting fires again, Tune?" *She's such a fireball. I'm going to miss her.*

"No, but let me tell you about the fire that lit up Spifry," exclaimed Antuna.

Spifry, a little embarrassed, jumped in, "Another time, Tune. Let's hear why Dinomite asked us here."

"Okay, Dino, what's up?" asked Antuna, anxious to hear what restrictions might affect their friendship.

Dinomite inched toward Beegan and Beebie. "First, let me say hello to the bee sisters here. Hi girls, I sure missed your fuzzy coats." He wanted to distract them—else they too quickly get on the subject that he dodged as much as he avoided water. *This circumstance is painful for me in more ways than one.*

"Oh Dino, you're gonna make us blush," buzzed Beebie.

"How've ya been, you crazy white ant?" asked Beegan, as the twins closed in on Dinomite, giving him a double bee hug.

Dinomite was delighted at the attention, but when he felt a warmth rush through him, a reminder of their special friendship, he knew he had to get right to the point. *If I don't bring it up now, maybe I never will.* "Not so good. Guess you know they called me up for duty. My youthful hexays are over." *Things will never be the same for us.*

"Yes, we heard," replied Spifry slowly. "We feel awful for you."

Dinomite marched to the left and then back to the right. "Don't feel bad. I like military life." But then, everything about his chipper expression changed. "But it's hard not seeing your friends." *Especially Antuna, my savior.*

Dinomite enjoyed life as a soldier. Having lost his parents and most of his termite community when the bough crushed his mound, he saw his platoon mates as his new family.

Antuna trembled, and a tear dropped from her eye. "I guess you can't come by anymore. Or do you get some furloughs?"

Dinomite quavered. "No, they don't want me seeing other insects anymore." *It's not fair, but it's my new life.*

"So, this is goodbye?" sniffled Beebie.

"I'm afraid so," gulped Dinomite. *It hurts to lose my friends, but I like where I'm going.*

"Well, let's not make it such a sad goodbye, everyone," insisted Spifry. "Let's remember the good times."

"Like when Dinomite interviewed Beetlebob and brought back the strong sap for us to try," exclaimed Antuna. "I wish we had some now."

"How about when we first met Dino, and Tune scolded him for going swimming," chimed Beegan.

Right then, six of Dinomite's termite platoon-mates stormed into the open log. Dinomite first saw his close buddy Armite, who he had asked to contact Beegan.

"What's going on, Armie?" questioned Dinomite. "I told you to keep this secret." *I don't understand.*

Armite confessed with a feeble fragrance before Bigmite entered the log. "Bigmite insisted I tell him where you went. Everyone's gonna get slapped down if any of us are late for curfew. So, he said we had to come here right away and bring you back on time."

Dinomite knew Bigmite was a large termite, almost twice his size, with an ego that matched his physique. Although a recruit, he used his size to dominate many of his platoon mates. Bigmite tried his best to reach the top of the pecking order among his peers. Dinomite detested his arrogance and resisted following Bigmite at any cost. He gravitated toward inspiring, creative leaders, not those that used brute strength and coercion to yield power. *I know they follow Bigmite, not because they respect him, but because he is intimidating.*

Then Bigmite pointed to Antuna and released a solid stench. "Let the others go, but get that ant."

"What are you talking about? I'll come right now," pleaded Dinomite. *I hate they follow this brute!*

"We're gonna bring the ant prisoner back with us and show Sargemite what we do to their kind," insisted Bigmite, who

Dinomite knew hated him almost as much as he despised ants. "It's our only case if we're late."

Two of the termites rushed in and grabbed Antuna, who struggled and kicked them both very hard. They stumbled back, surprised at her zeal. Both Beegan and Beebie sprang up next to Antuna and threatened the termites with their stingers.

"Touch her again, and you are shish ka-bee," barked Beegan with her stinger exposed.

As two more termite soldiers approached Beegan and Beebie from behind, Spifry screamed, "Watch out!" He then spat at one termite, knocking him down and stunning him.

"Okay, kill 'em all!" Bigmite yelled as he lunged forward towards the bees.

Dinomite noted that the other termites froze, shocked by an order they never expected. *Here's my chance.* And before anyone even saw him move, he toppled Bigmite to the ground. *They're not taking Antuna or any of my friends.*

With his jaws open around Bigmite's neck, he hissed loud and clear, "Nobody's killing anyone around here unless Bigmite wants to go first." A volatile vapor permeated the air.

Knowing that Dinomite had him in a death-bite grip, Bigmite groveled, "No Dinomite, please. I'll do whatever you say. Spare me to-hexay, and I'll always do what you ask."

"Get out of here with your cronies and let me say goodbye to my friends," snarled Dinomite. Then, as the other termites scrambled out of the open log, he released Bigmite and told him, "I'll hold you to that promise. And make sure no one tells anyone what happened here tonight." *If you don't, I'll snap my jaws next time.*

Whiter than any termite that hadn't just molted, Bigmite

skulked out of the log, whimpering, "I will, uh, I mean, we won't, I promise."

When Bigmite left, Dinomite turned to his friends and said, "Bigmite has always been a jerk, and I'm glad I got to put him in his place." Bile rose in his throat as he thought of him. "The other guys are okay and would do anything for me. But I'd better go if I want to make curfew." *I hope I see you again.*

※ ※ ※

Back at the colony, Beegan and Beebie were more reserved than usual. Although they were careful not to spread the story that Spifry fried Spifrida, they talked about how Beebie and Antuna got caught and escaped from a spider web. This narrative reinforced many other stories about ants and other colony insects recently seized by spiders. The spider's bellies were no longer full, and they were hunting again.

Realizing that spiders were creating trouble, Genant met with his top Major about the growing threat and asked Assistant for a report.

Major Assistant summarized the circumstances to his superior. "Commander Genant, the spiders are on the prowl again. We've been losing many colony insects."

"Yes, Major, we can't have them so nearby that they can attack us at will," asserted Genant. *I knew this threat would come, but I'll get to test my troops.*

Assistant inched closer to Genant. "What do you propose we should do about it?"

"We have to banish them from the colony and drive them out near the new lands," replied Genant, voicing his long-awaited desire.

"Are you sure we can force them back?" questioned Assistant.

Genant was confident in his assessment. "Yes, we're more aggressive and cunning, and we can out-smart them." *Bring it on. I can't wait.*

Indeed, this supposition accurately reflected both the ants' characteristics and Genant's preparations.

"Do you have something specific in mind?" asked Assistant.

Genant explained his strategy, which he had considered since the insects arrived on their new planet. "Yes, starting tomorrow, have our soldier ants go out early each morning to raid the nests of mothering spiders. We'll destroy the eggs or massacre the tiny babies as they hatch."

"Yes, that is very shrewd, Commander," responded Assistant. "We should use teams of six ants, and they can spray the mother with formic acid, and it will paralyze her."

Genant sneered. "Yes, tear the mother to pieces and use more formic acid to burn the eggs." An ominous odor saturated the ether. *Spider baby mush—I can see it now.*

"We may lose one or two soldiers," continued Assistant. "But we'll destroy hundreds of eggs with each raid."

Genant boasted, "The General knows what's best. So, we'll get them where they nest!"

When the raids started, the mother spiders were not passive and butchered a few ants while defending their young. On their own, though, they could not guard against the several ants Genant used in the raids. Scytodes or spitting spiders ejected a venom-laced, gluey thread from their fangs that stunned and ensnared their prey. Spitting was an offensive technique used to trap a single insect on or off the web, but it was also a defensive tactic. However, it was not a strategy that succeeded when many nasty ants attacked a spider. Spimadam, the commander of the spider army, knew surviving mother spiders were distraught at the prospect of losing their babies. So, it did not surprise her when they demanded swift retaliatory action.

In response to Genant's aggressive tactics, Spimadam arranged a strategic conference with her top officer, Spima, and asked for an update.

Spima solicited advice on the matter. "Spimadam, Genant's soldiers have been attacking our nests, and the mother spiders are panicking."

"I know, but the mothers need to be more aggressive," asserted Spimadam. "The ants are going after our young. We must set our spit to kill and not stun!" *Ants will never pose a significant threat to us superior spiders.*

Spimadam could sense Spima's desperation, detecting a flaky fragrance. "They are trying, but many ants are attacking them," Spima replied. "And these ants spray formic acid."

"Yes, but we can spit our venom at them from a distance," responded Spimadam. *I refuse to accept that ants can defeat us.*

"That works for one or two ants, but not the half dozen they use in the raids," countered Spima.

"I assume the ants attack nesting mothers because they avoid our webs." *Perhaps we need additional defensive tactics.*

"Yes, that's what's happening, ma'am," agreed Spima.

"Okay, urge our soldiers off the webs and have them ambush the raiding ants," ordered Spimadam, resorting to a time-tested strategy that worked well for individual spiders on the hunt. "We will force the ants to quit once they feel our burning spit!"

Although Spimadam thought she had an excellent plan,

spiders were solitary hunters, so it went against their nature. Indeed, spiders were not immune to the practice of killing each other for a good meal. They were almost blind and caught their prey relying on insect locomotor vibrations. Although this technique was ideal for catching a meal, it did not work well in an ambush and failed even worse after Genant discovered what they were doing.

On learning of the new spider maneuvers, Assistant met again with Genant. "Commander Genant, it seems the spiders are organizing their best spitters to ambush our raiding parties," he reported.

"Don't worry, Major, this tactic is not something they trained for, and I have some ideas that will quash their attempts," replied Genant.

Assistant was curious about the new plan. "Yes? I am all antennae, Commander."

"First, have some of our strongest minds join the raiders," explained Genant. "Double the party with six sprayers and six telepaths. And have the ants use triangular formations."

"Please explain further. I am not sure how that will help." *I don't doubt Genant, but I need some clarification on the workings behind the scheme.*

"These spiders are almost blind, and they spit instinctively wherever they detect movement," clarified Genant. "With a triangular formation, many spiders will blow their wad on the lead ant."

"Clever, sir, but what about the telepaths?" asked Assistant. *I don't understand. How could they possibly help?*

Although ruthless to his enemies, Assistant could tell that Genant was tolerant and patient with his underlings.

"Recall that our best ant transporters could carry up to five thousand times their weight on Earth," started Genant. "This is not because they are stronger than you or me. It's because they use telepathy to move the load. Here on Poo-ponic, the gravity is ten times less than Earth, so our best telepaths can now lift objects fifty thousand times their weight." He winked at his underling. "I call it an arthropod mind-trick."

"That is amazing, but how does this help in battle?" puzzled Assistant. *I am enthusiastic about learning from the master.*

Genant swung his forelimbs as if tossing something. "I selected the soldiers with the best telepathic skills for a special squad, and I have been training them to not only lift but throw objects."

"So, they can hurl sticks and stones to crush the spiders?" *I think I get it.*

Genant explained further, "Yes, but they can also just fling stones everywhere, and the spiders will spit at the vibrations they make when they hit the ground."

"I see. We only need to pitch stones to shake the ground all about. Then, they'll spit everywhere and take each other out," offered Assistant. *I knew it. This ant is a genius.*

"Well said, Major, you are an excellent study. There will be lots of spider friendly fire. And when they're stunned or have wasted their shot, we'll spray, jump, and tear them apart," replied Genant. Assistant detected a brassy bouquet emanating from his superior.

Genant's plans were highly effective, and the spider ambushes were abysmal. Assistant was pleased to report that more and more spider mothers and young fell prey to their acid attacks. He could tell that everyone in the spider community was shocked at their army's ineptitude and feared that their family would be the next one dissolved alive. Assistant was jubilant when Spimadam and the spiders retreated to the lands outside the colony.

While supervising a final deadly raid, Assistant overheard Spimadam's lament. "We are losing too many sisters and brothers and even more babies and mothers. We must leave this place before we all taste their mace."

With that, Genant, Assistant, and their raiding parties banished the spiders from the colony. Most spiders survived but lived in outlying areas, still within the original Earth Island but outside the colony border.

🐜 🐜 🐜

Antuna, Beegan, and Beebie met Spifry one last time before the banishment. Antuna tried to drum up support for an anti-banishment movement, but the idea of crossing Genant terrified everyone. They also felt the spiders were getting off easy. They would no longer have access to the marsh, but they didn't like fungi, anyway. If they wanted to quench their thirst, they could drink at other wetlands beyond the Earth Island. They would also be further from their food sources, but as insects were the critical item on their menu, the colony members had no problem with the arrangement.

"Spifry, we tried to stop the exile, but there was no support for our pleas," cried Antuna. *It's hopeless, and even I can't stop it.* She feared so deeply for Spifry's life that she could not hide the terror in her voice.

"I expected that, but thanks for trying," sighed Spifry.

"What will you do, Fry?" fretted Beebie.

Spifry stood tall and puffed himself up to show off his enhanced physique. "You likely see I've had a growth spurt these last few hexths, and my leaders noticed. When word got out that I was the one that fried Spifrida, I thought I'd get in trouble, but I got drafted. It seems the army is expanding in case the colony insects attack us again."

"But what will you eat?" sniveled Beegan, realizing that banishment would separate Spifry from his food source.

"Oh, don't worry, the spider army takes care of its own," Spifry seeped a soothing scent.

"We're going to miss you, Fry," declared Antuna. *I can't believe I'm losing another friend.* Then, all too suddenly, her memory flooded with thoughts of Dinomite, and her sadness grew.

"Me too, but when you gotta go, you gotta go," replied Spifry, trying to make light of the matter.

Spifry gave each of his three closest friends a multi-legged hug. Then he turned and scuttled away.

"Goodbye, my octa-limbed friend," Antuna murmured. *I must hold back my tears.*

※ ※ ※

After expelling the spiders from the colony, Genant turned his attention to termites. Both ants and termites were social species, but as shown by Dinomite's early interview and the actions of his platoon-mates, they were only friends with other termites and suspected other insects. The ants were amiable with other insects that did not eat or compete with them. However, they often took over things, so their best relationships were with other insects that like to follow. Termites hated to follow directions from other insects, especially ants, who competed for the same food.

A short while later, Beebie and Beegan flew to Antuna when they saw her entering her nest.

Antuna cracked a big smile and congratulated them. "You guys started to-hexay, didn't you? So how did your first foraging trip go?"

"It was great. We even did a waggle dance when we got back to tell the others where to go," Beebie gushed. *I finally realized my life's calling.*

"We located tons of flowers at the eastern end of Earth Island," Beegan crowed. "There were even some flowers growing in the new lands."

"That's great. I am so happy for you!" exclaimed Antuna.

Beegan waddled close to Antuna. "But Tune, we have to tell you what we heard from some of the other foragers."

Although bees were friendly and wouldn't hurt a fly or other insect unless provoked, they gossiped. A favorite expression among bees was *what's the buzz*, which meant, *do you have any good dirt?*

"Oh, I am all antennae. What's the fuzzy buzz?" cackled Antuna.

Beebie jumped in, thrilled to spread gossip, "It's about Genant and the termites." *I expect you'll never guess.*

Antuna bounced up and down in response. "Tell me already!"

"Back on Earth, a pack of termites killed Genant's father," described Beebie. "He has despised termites ever since. So, our foraging team worked with a group of flies last hexek. And one of them said that Genant asked the commander of the fly reconnaissance squad, Flyhi, to double up their surveillance of the movements of the termites." *How about that? You can't beat my gossiping skills.*

"Whatever for?" queried Antuna, now still as a stalked praying mantis.

"One of our fellow foragers said she heard Flyhi tell Genant that termites were having secret talks with the spiders," expanded Beegan. "He said the spiders wanted the termites to supply them with the corpses of any ants or bees in our morgues."

"I don't understand. What would be in it for the termites?" puzzled Antuna.

Beegan scanned around and excreted a subdued scent, "Seems they agreed spiders wouldn't spit at any termites out foraging in return for some dead ants and bees."

"Our bee spy said Flyhi told Genant that the termites even promised to inform the spiders when they heard about any teams of ants that were going out foraging," interjected Beebie. *I bet you can't top that.* "That way, they could get some live meat, too."

"Now that's some gossip, girls," gushed Antuna. "Do they know what Genant is going to do about it?"

Beebie could tell Antuna was worried about the implications of his actions for termites and their dear friend Dino. *I expect she knows that Dino may have to fight.*

"Genant wants his fly spies to observe some termites supplying the spiders with bodies or more information about ant movements," said Beebie with the flare of a dragonfly swooping down over the water to snare its prey. "He hopes to catch them in the act."

"How do they know all this?" pondered Antuna. "Wouldn't Genant and Flyhi keep this hush-hush?"

Beegan edged very close to Antuna, dribbling a babbling bouquet. "Genant secretly met Flyhi in a thick patch of grapevines on the far side of the fly palm-tree jungle. They thought they were alone, but one bee from our group was deep down in a nearby hollyhock collecting nectar. She sat tight and heard every juicy bit."

"Wow, she heard it through the grapevine," exclaimed Antuna.

"You know what happens when you put a bunch of female bees together," hooted Beebie. "We were buzzing up a storm," she said. *What a day! We snagged not only nectar, but some sweet gossip.*

※ ※ ※

After a few hexths of failing to catch termites colluding with spiders, Genant gave up on that tact. Instead, he prevented termites from foraging in areas where the spiders congregated. When the termites resisted the command, Genant ordered the termites to cease expeditions. Termites defied the stay-in-the-colony order, and skirmishes broke out between the soldier ants and the wandering termites. When Genant threatened martial law and put many termites under burrow arrest, the termites revolted. The General of the termites, Bitemite, initially instructed his mates to stage dig-ins and work stoppages. When he heard about the impending martial law, he flipped his antenna and planned to start an all-out rebellion.

Hearing about Bitemite's anger, the bee sisters again approached Antuna as she collected some fungi at the marsh's edge.

"Hi Beegan and Beebie, did you get lots of nectar to-hexay?" Antuna extended her antennae towards the bees.

"No, but we got a lot more good dirt," replied Beebie, who was proud to have more news.

"What's the buzz?" implored Antuna. *I hope this isn't more bad news for Dino.*

Beegan beamed. "Remember when we told you why Genant hates termites? Well, now we got the scoop on Bitemite."

Antuna shuffled from side to side. "Don't keep me in suspense, girls. Tell me already." *I can't wait.*

"Well, Bitemite lost his mother and an uncle in a squabble with ants over aphids and the honeydew they produced," started Beebie.

"Over aphids?" Antuna puzzled. *I don't believe it.*

"Yes, an ant colony had a herd of aphids, and they milked honeydew from them by rubbing their abdomens," explained Beebie.

"My father and I used to do that," exclaimed Antuna, pleased to reminisce about a cherished experience with her father. "Honeydew is so sweet, and the aphids loved it when we rubbed their tummies with our antennae." *Maybe now I see.*

Beebie shook rapidly and wiped her hind limbs over her wings to clean off some pollen. "Sounds like a perfect partnership."

Antuna smiled. "Yeah, we massaged them, and they excreted all we could eat. Everyone was glad." Her grin waned. *I miss the old hexays.*

"But what exactly is honeydew?" asked Beegan.

Antuna grimaced. "It's gross, but they suck sap from the phloem sacs of flowering plants." *I can't wait till they hear this.* "It's the sugary stuff that makes nectar, and we eat the honeydew when they poop it out."

"If it tastes anything like nectar, I can see why you'd milk those little critters." Beebie laughed. "And I wouldn't care what end it came from."

"Exactly, but let's get back to Bitemite!" urged Antuna. *Tell me what this means for Dino.*

"The termites fed all winter on the small bush where the

aphids lived," explained Beegan. "They damaged it so much that the aphids left to find another bush in the spring."

Beebie flailed her limbs around. "Yeah, and when the ants discovered their friendly aphids had left, they were angry."

"What did they do?" asked Antuna. *Don't tell me they slaughtered them all.*

"They attacked the termites and killed Bitemite's mother and uncle in a massive fight," expounded Beegan.

Beebie buzzed her wings. "And now Bitemite is fuming about Genant's proposed martial law," she continued, "bringing the old grudge back to the present."

"Sounds like they're going to resist harder, and he might do something crazy," concluded Beegan.

A rambling reek dispersed, and Antuna responded, "That's not good." *So much for Beefirst's plan for a cooperative insect society, and what about Dino? I haven't seen him in hexths.*

CHAPTER 4

FRIENDSHIP LOST

Does not amity emit one's style?

With rays of tenderness, humor, or beguile.

That may be eclipsed when faced with trial.

When shining love dims by defile,

and darkness prevails with much revile.

CAPTAIN SLIMITE AND his immediate supervisor, Major Mostmite, joined a tête-à-tête with their commander, General Bitemite. Slimite respected the General, but like Mostmite, he disliked Bitemite.

The General stared at Mostmite. "Major, I brought you here because I want you to create a crack team of our best fighters."

Mostmite raised his eyebrows. "Are you planning something to stop Genant's martial law?"

"Yes. Does Genant think termites will follow his rule

just because ants are ruthless?" replied Bitemite, spewing a scratchy stink.

"Of course not," replied Mostmite. "His rules are ridiculous. So, what do you propose?"

Slimite remained silent. *I know I should only speak when asked a question.*

"We need to execute a coup to get rid of that evil commander, Genant," exclaimed Bitemite. "If we remain in this colony, we need a termite in charge of the inter-insect military command."

"I assume you would like to take over as commander?" surmised Mostmite. "I endorse that wholeheartedly. We can't trust ants to treat us fairly."

Bitemite continued, "Captain Slimite, I brought you in because I want you to help Mostmite identify the best soldiers for this mission."

"Yes, sir, General Bitemite, I am honored to help the Major," Slimite replied honestly, although it was a rarity for him to tell the truth. *I'll do anything to work towards my promotion.*

Bitemite looked up from his scroll and smiled. "By the way, I heard about this recruit, Dinomite, who fights like a velociraptor. I know he's inexperienced, but I want him on the team. Put him in your unit so that you can monitor him."

"Yes sir, excellent sir," agreed Slimite. "I know him." *That kid, I hope you're kidding.* "The recruiters assigned him to my training unit. I assume you heard he took down another conscript twice his size in a fight over a girl?" *I'm guessing you don't know it was an ant!*

"Yes, and we'll need soldiers with that kind of grit for this operation," said Bitemite.

Slimite didn't tell the general that after hearing about his fight with Bigmite to save an ant, he enrolled Dinomite in an intensive mind-warping program to instill an intense hatred of ants. Although he expected that Dinomite still had lingering feelings for Antuna, Slimite knew the program had planted the seeds in him to despise ants as evil enemy combatants.

🐜 🐜 🐜

To reward the termites that joined Bitemite's clandestine team, the captains promised them a furlough for a few hexays before they started training for the mission. Dinomite used his time-off to arrange another rendezvous with Antuna and the bee sisters at the hollowed-out log. He was conflicted and partly wanted to party with his old friends. But he planned to end their relationship altogether. So Dinomite met them on the second hexay of his leave, which he discovered was the bee sisters' hexay off.

Antuna and the bee sisters arrived at the log at the appointed time, just before mid-hexay.

Antuna spotted Dino on top of the log, chewing on some loose sawdust. "Dino, I can't believe you called us here again. Won't you get in trouble?"

"No, my mates and my sergeants were so impressed when the brass picked me for an elite fighting team," swanked Dinomite. "No one mistrusts me or questions my where-abouts." *I don't get in trouble anymore.*

"That's great, Dino. Do you know what the mission will be?" asked Beebie.

"No, they haven't told us yet, but it's hush-hush," scoffed Dinomite. "I'm not allowed to tell you, even if I knew." He directed the others into the hollow log to continue their conversation. *We'd better not speak in the open.*

"Beegan and Beebie have been telling me some strange

stories they heard about Genant and termite surveillance," started Antuna cautiously, hoping for some clarity. "Do you think it has something to do with that?"

"I don't know," derided Dinomite. "I have heard nothing about spying on termites. But I wouldn't put it past that evil ant, general." *I know ants are the worst.*

Beegan puffed herself up and looked Dinomite straight in the eye. "Genant thinks termites are conspiring with spiders against the ants."

"That's crazy talk," challenged Dinomite, radiating a ratty reek. "Where did you learn that?" *Genant's a tyrant, and you don't need to tell me that.*

"It's something we heard in the field," divulged Beebie, oozing a funky fragrance.

Dinomite openly frowned at Beebie, making his distaste for the accusation clear. "Don't believe everything you hear from a bunch of gossipy old bee-hens." *Especially if the source was an ant, I'd say.*

"Anyway, take care of yourself," countered Antuna. "We don't want you getting your head taken off in some stupid battle over old hatreds."

Dinomite relaxed his tense muscles a little. "Yes, I've heard the stories about the wicked ants that massacred Bitemite's kin. And I've heard about Genant's gripes too." *Tell me something I don't know.*

Antuna lowered her head. "I thought Beefirst's plans and our cooperation after the Great Displacement would change that. I am afraid our planet is in great peril we can't belie, and if we keep carrying old grudges, we all will die."

"The way things are, we're better off keeping to our own

kind," concluded Dinomite. *I've learned that recently.* "Face it, termites and ants don't mix, except you, Tune."

"That settles it. Female bees should rule Poo-ponic!" crowed Beegan, trying to diffuse the tension in the air.

"Yeah, Sis, you got that right," gloated Beebie.

"Touché," supported Dinomite. *I don't believe it, but it's an excellent diversion.*

"Well, we're so glad we got to see you again," added Antuna, with a hopeful sway in her voice. "I hope we can meet again after your secret mission."

Dinomite abruptly headed out the open end of the log and chirped, "Bye girls, see you when I can." *But let me tell you—don't hold your breath.*

Beegan remarked as she and Beebie flew Antuna back to the colony, "He was a little cool there when he left. No hugs or long goodbyes."

"I expect he didn't want to think it could be the last good-bye," Antuna sniffled, then paused for a long moment to consider the possibility. "Whether it be by force or by choice."

Antuna already suspected that Dinomite wanted to cool their friendship, but she vowed never to abandon her friend, no matter how distant he became. He was family to her, no matter what.

❊ ❊ ❊

Dinomite trained for three hexeks with two hundred termite troops involved in the mission. They each went through various types of training, not knowing what their ultimate tasks would be. Dinomite's team captain said they wouldn't assign exact duties until two to three hexays before the operation. Dinomite also continued his mind-warping program, which was more intensive, and his mistrust and hatred of ants grew. But Dinomite questioned the treatment he got from the captains of the mission.

"Sarge, I feel that Captain Slimite and the other captains on this assignment don't like me very much," declared Dinomite. *Despite achieving all my goals, I've received many minor reprimands from my superiors.*

Sargemite, also on the mission, gave Dinomite a stern, hard look. "Work hard and don't worry about it. They don't need to like you. They only need to know you're doing your job."

"My teammates say it's how they treat all rookies," continued Dinomite. *It's got to be that. I've worked so hard.*

Sargemite edged closer to Dinomite and lowered his voice. "Let me be straight with you, private. You're young, and some captains think the brass should have picked a more seasoned soldier." He scowled at his charge. "It seems Commander Bitemite wanted you, but those under him did not."

Dinomite squirmed, but stood his ground close to Sargemite. "I know I'm young, but I'm working hard. And I'm in step with the others." *It's not fair to me.*

Sargemite glared back at him. "They also think you're an ant-lover. And you took the place of one of their claw-picked veteran fighters, who hates ants."

"I don't love ants anymore," exclaimed Dinomite. *Ants are evil, and I have no ant friends.* "Give me a chance, and I'll prove it."

Sargemite blinked and backed away. "Well, excel at both your physical and mental training. Then they'll see it and realize your strength of character."

Dinomite stretched to full attention. "I'll work twice as hard. There'll be no better soldier than me, I promise." And then, without controlling it, he imagined the various ways he could take down an ant: with a crushing body slam or with his pincers after a mesmerizing claw spring or a full-frontal rolling attack.

Sargemite smiled, sensing a wily whiff from his recruit.

✺ ✺ ✺

Meanwhile, Antuna continued to worry about her friend Dino. She fretted about Dinomite ever since they said goodbye to him. But her concern peaked in recent hexays since she had a feeling his mission was about to happen.

Antuna approached the bee sisters just before they were about to leave on another foraging run. "Girls, I'm worried about Dino. I thought his undertaking would happen soon." *I am so concerned.* "Then I realized what I called his mission, and I saw it *will* be an *undertaking*, with Dinomite going straight to the morgue." She frowned. "We gotta get him out of this!" A sulking smell filled the air.

"I don't know if there's anything we can do," declared Beegan. "Dino seems very keen on his mission."

"But he might die!" cried Antuna. *I've seen it. He'll burn in agony.*

"What if we told him Tune got lost in the jungle, and he has to help find her," suggested Beebie.

"He'll never buy that." Beegan sighed. "He knows Tune has no reason to wander far from her nest."

"I know! One of you could give him a message that I am sick," suggested Antuna. "Tell him I'm dying of a fungal infection from a bad batch of fungi at the marsh." *My fungi farm, our fungi farm. He and I built it together.*

"I get it," chimed Beebie. "Dino saw how proud you were

of the fungi farm after your science project. So, he won't suspect anything."

"Bingo, Beebie!" gushed Antuna. *I'm happy Beebie gleaned my intent.*

"But how can we get him the news?" puzzled Beegan.

Antuna gave Beegan one of her *do it, don't screw it* looks. "You should fly to the regular termite training base and ask for Bigmite." Antuna explained further, "And remind him he said he'd do anything for Dino." *I know it will work.*

Beegan interjected, "I'll pretend I'm a messenger. And I'll get him to send a message to Dino that you're dying."

Beebie sighed, not entirely on board with the plan, but she felt like they had limited choices. "It sounds a little risky, but what else can we do?"

Antuna stared off for a heavy moment, drifting back to the simpler days of their youth. *I wish we could be friends again, with nothing else to do.* Time was changing everything, and she inwardly wished it to slow down.

❦ ❦ ❦

The next hexay after her nectar collection duties, Beegan flew to the termite barracks and sought Bigmite. She pretended she was an apprentice in a new program that trained bees to work as messengers to help the flies. Beebie even sewed her a banner like the flies wore to show they were official messengers. The plot worked because soldiers always responded well to stripes or badges, making them seem official. Beegan wasted no time and gave Bigmite the message about Antuna.

Bigmite stared long at Beegan and remarked, "I told Dinomite I would do anything for him, not his fuzzy-headed friends." *Does she take me for a fool?*

Beegan puffed herself up and sprinkled a sharp scent. "Well, how do you think Dinomite will take it when Antuna dies before he can see her again because you wouldn't relay my message?"

Bigmite grumbled in response. "Well, when you put it like that, I can try to find a way." *But I still hate bees.*

"You had better, or I'm sure Dinomite will have you by the throat again," said Beegan.

"Yes, ma'am," shrugged Bigmite. "But this is the only time I'll do anything for a lousy bee."

Although Bigmite recoiled at the mention of Dinomite, he was still a formidable termite. Embarrassed by the rumors about him losing a fight to Dinomite, he became extra nasty with many other soldiers he encountered, even the officers. So, when any soldier told him they couldn't get his message through to Dinomite because of the sensitive nature of the mission, he reminded them how much bigger he was than them. Then, when he realized that the soldiers at the next station hampered him, he found out who caused the roadblock and visited them. He went right to the secret training grounds, where he met with Dinomite's captain.

"So, private, I hear you are a very persuasive soldier," jeered Captain Slimite as Bigmite approached.

"Yes sir, captain sir, I have my ways," boasted Bigmite. *And I'll coax you too.*

Slimite gave him a mocking glare. "You lost your *way* coming here, and what makes you think private Dinomite is even here?"

"I was told..." started Bigmite. His confidence shook. *This task may not be so easy, I think.*

"That's *sir, I was told*, private. Do you think I care what you were told?" derided Slimite. "I could have you court-mangled for the act you pulled. Sit down!" An acrid aroma inundated the area.

"But I…"

Slimite stood up and stared down at Bigmite, who was now seated. "That's *But, sir*, private. Do you even have any training?" Slimite mocked further, "I know you like to throw your weight around, but nobody intimidates me, soldier."

Bigmite squirmed under pressure. "But sir, Dino's friend is…"

"Private, I don't care about Dinomite's friend. And I already heard the story," barked Slimite.

Bigmite shriveled in his chair, realizing that his size would not influence this officer. He cast him a frown. *How can I crack this nut?*

Slimite smirked, "Private, I don't want you to think I'm doing you any favors."

"Sir?" Bigmite raised his eyebrows. *So, I get to you after all?*

"Dinomite is a good soldier, twice the soldier you are. But he's young, and he's in over his head. So, I want him out of here."

Bigmite perked up and sat forward in his chair. "I beg your pardon, sir, but why can't you just turf him out?" *Cause he'd slide through your slippery claws, I'm guessing.*

"Because General Bitemite likes him. Ever since he heard the story about how he took you down," bellowed Slimite.

"I see, sir," groveled Bigmite. *I'll never live that down.*

"But this circumstance might give me the ammo I need," sneered Slimite. "So, I'm going to let you give him your message. And then I don't want to see your sorry hindgut ever again!"

❧ ❧ ❧

When Dinomite got the news about Antuna's illness, he was

distraught. He wanted to rush to her side on one claw, but he desired to leave his past behind him on the other claw. He didn't want to show any weakness in his developing hatred of ants, and there was no way to get the leave, anyway. He had nearly finished his training. Sargemite said that the major would pass out their specific assignments at a meeting after the solar star rising tomorrow. *This appointment is such a fantastic opportunity for me. I can't leave now, no matter who is dying.* And though he didn't want to believe it, the thought crossed his mind that Antuna might try to trick him into quitting the army. But he didn't let the idea linger long, deciding that there's no way that Beegan would say the marsh fungi made her sick unless it was true. *But what if she dies? She is the one that saved my life. What if I could help her now? I hate her. How could she put me in this position?* His own suffocating scent overtook him.

Dinomite's troop had been through the most arduous exercise of the entire training period over the last twelve hexours, and Dinomite had not slept more than a hexour in two hexays. When curfew came, there were only three hexours before reveille, and Dinomite could only toss and turn, perseverating on the same thoughts. Dinomite flopped into a deep sleep hexutes before the sergeants came into the barracks to raise the troops. All the other soldiers arose immediately, eager to attend the meeting to get their assignments. Dinomite's bunkmates and Sargemite could not rouse him. When one of his friends told the sergeant that Dinomite hated water, Sargemite ordered the corporal to get a pail to splash him.

Right then, Captain Slimite arrived and ordered the corporal to stop. "At ease, corporal, let the boy sleep. He got some hard news yester-hexay, and I'm sure he needs the rest."

Sargemite couldn't believe the order rendered and

questioned the captain, "But sir, doesn't he need to attend the assignment meeting?"

Slimite replied with a lie, "I've got his orders here. I'll tell him when he wakes."

The corporal and Sargemite were now trailing the other soldiers who had left to go to the pre-breakfast assignment meeting. It pleased them when Captain Slimite relieved them of their reveille duties, and they rushed out of the barracks.

～ ～ ～

Major Mostmite, a young, up-and-coming officer, presided over the assignment meeting. He was a hot-tempered officer who climbed the ranks by stepping hard on the backs of the soldiers under his command. No one ever crossed Mostmite without paying the price. When Mostmite called out Dinomite's name to give him his orders, and no one appeared, Mostmite fumed like an old sequoia struck by lightning.

After the meeting, Mostmite commanded Slimite and Sargemite to come to his chambers. Sargemite quivered and said nothing during the brief encounter.

Mostmite stood up and yelled to Slimite, "What is the meaning of this, Captain? A private under your watch, sleeping through an assignment meeting."

After throwing a nasty glance at Sargemite, Slimite, true to his name, smiled and cast a shadowy scent. "Sir, if I may explain, this Private Dinomite has been a problem throughout the training. To-hexay was the third time he slept through reveille. After his second offense, I warned him he'd be off the mission if it happened again." Slimite continued his deceit. "So, when he was late again this morning, I told him I would return him to his regular outfit. I apologize. I didn't inform you. But there was no time with the rush to the pre-breakfast meeting." *I hope this works.*

The major softened his tone. "It's just as well. I was never too pleased when General Bitemite insisted we assign a young private to such an important mission."

Slimite sat down in a chair by Mostmite's desk. "Yes, Major, I agree." *Good, I think he fell for it.*

Mostmite motioned for Sargemite to sit down. "I also got my orders to-hexay. I am to attend a diplomatic event involving the ants and the bees on the other side of the colony. Bitemite wants to deflect attention away from our mission here and has organized some inter-insect trilateral meeting with Queen Beefirst in attendance."

"You'll miss the action, sir?" asked Slimite. *I know that will rile him up.*

"Yes, dang it, but you know what they say about majors, don't you?"

I know this one. Slimite lied again. "No, sir, what is that?"

Mostmite perked up and delivered his line, "Being a major is great, but a general is finer. Do the general's petty jobs, and don't forget you're the minor."

"Haha, excellent sir," replied Slimite. *I never miss the chance to suck up to a superior.*

"Since I must cross the colony, I could take that private with me and give him a good talking to," suggested Mostmite. "I'll scare the sleeping disorder right out of him."

After throwing another scowl at Sargemite, Slimite deceived for the third time. "Can't do it, sir. He's already gone. I shipped him out myself, bunk and all." *I'm on my game.*

Mostmite blasted a laugh. "Bunk and all, good one, Captain. Haha, you're dismissed."

As they left Mostmite's chamber, Slimite gave Sargemite the rest of the hexay off and thanked him for his loyalty. Then, he awakened and dismissed Dinomite, sending him back to his regular unit after scolding him and demoting him from private first class back to private. Although he assumed Sargemite liked him, it surprised Slimite that the records showed his sergeant never supported him when asked for recommendations for his potential promotions.

🐜 🐜 🐜

Although Genant's fly spies uncovered no covert encounters between termites and spiders, they noticed a colossal termite soldier who trekked from the regular termite training site to the beetle's sequoia grove south of the ant burrow. They tracked him to a thick patch of forest and, on careful inspection, noticed that there were many termites in the forest conducting a training exercise.

Flyhi reported the suspicious activity to Genant, who became livid when he heard the news.

Jumping up out of his seat, Genant interrogated Flyhi. "Are you telling me that the termites are colluding with the beetles and not spiders?" *I can't believe it!*

Flyhi stood at attention. "No, we never saw termites interacting with beetles, and the beetles ignored them."

"But what could they be doing there in secret behind our nest?" He emitted a foggy fragrance. *I hate those slimy termites.*

"I don't know, Genant, but they were training hard. It was an elite group of their best soldiers," offered Flyhi.

Genant waved his limbs and cleared the surrounding air. "Best soldiers, behind our burrow. I know what's going on! Bitemite has finally lost it." He jumped out of his chair. "He thinks they can attack the ant burrow and take control of my command." *I'll kill that nasty white ant myself.*

"It looks that way, General."

"Major Assistant warned me this might happen if I implemented martial law," Genant surmised. "Well, thank you, Flyhi. I assume you'll keep our conversation confidential." He paused, then continued, "No, wait, could you have one of your team take a message from me to that scoundrel Bitemite?" *He'll freak when he discovers I'm on to him.*

"Of course, Genant, I take it you know flies are the most trustworthy of all insects," crowed Flyhi.

Indeed, this was a statement that even Genant would agree with, although he learned most bees and roaches were also very honorable, and worms were honest.

❧ ❧ ❧

Bitemite became disillusioned on reading the dispatch from Genant that he had discovered their secret mission. They no longer had the element of surprise, but that didn't dampen his enthusiasm. He sent a message back to Genant saying they would not surrender and planned to continue their training exercises. He knew Genant would not buy the story, that no plot was underway, and they were only training. But he was ready for a fight with his despised foe and prepared for Genant to attack. He called for reinforcements from the most senior platoon, older termites, but the ones with the most battle experience. He ordered Captain Slimite and Sergeant Sargemite to the front lines.

Captain Slimite started the skirmish with Sargemite at his side.

Slimite began, standing tall to impress his troops, "Sergeant, order the oldest termites to charge the ant front line. We need the hardened soldiers to begin the fight."

"Yes, sir," Sargemite replied, then addressed the troops, "Senior platoon advance and attack!" He swallowed hard. "Let's chop those ants up for dinner." *I'm sure this won't work.*

Half a hexour later, Slimite approached Sargemite to get an update. "Sergeant, report on the progress of our attack."

Sargemite shook a little as he spoke. "Captain, the senior platoon is suffering massive casualties. Should I have them retreat?" *I've told him the seniors are too old.*

"No, Sergeant, we need them to weaken the ant line so our elite team can follow and finish them off."

Sargemite trembled and continued, "But they're getting battered. They fight hard, but they're too old." *Why doesn't he ever listen to me?*

Slimite expounded, "Well, it's the way we always do it. They're the most experienced and the most expendable."

Unlike Genant, who was highly creative and would shift tactics to meet battle demands, Bitemite and his surrogates, including Slimite, always stuck to their traditional fighting techniques. They feared any changes were too risky and would likely lead to defeat. However, they also knew they had more significant numbers than Genant's forces and assumed this was all they needed to ensure victory.

"Should we send in the medics and bring back the wounded?" queried Sargemite. *They're all gonna die. I'd better bite my tongue.*

"No, General Bitemite didn't want medics. He's never used them before," barked Slimite.

Sargemite seeped a ruffled reek. "We better do something—the ants are advancing." *I think we're doomed.*

Still at attention, Slimite queried, "Is the elite team ready?"

"They're here, but they're terrified. The troops trained a lot, but many have never seen a battle like this." *I don't think he realizes how savage ants are.*

Now more agitated, Slimite roared out his command, "Well, motivate them, Sergeant. That's your job."

"Yes, sir," Sargemite replied, regaining his poise. Then, he again addressed the soldiers, "Okay, troops, look alive. Fight like your lives depend on it." *Because I know they do.* "Let's supplant these wimpy ants."

On the other side of the line, Major Assistant stood alongside Genant, directing the troops together.

"Major, our troops are doing well, but I want to see more jaws snapping and pincers pinching. I want limbs lopped off left and right," ordered Genant, strongly emphasizing each word.

"Yes, sir, there are no soldiers fiercer than our girls, and they hate termites," gloated Assistant. *I feed off Genant's calm demeanor.*

Genant reassured Assistant, "If our ants lose limbs, don't sweat it. Have the medics carry them back to the burrow—our nurses will lick their wounds. Their antifungal saliva will heal them so they can fight again." He looked over at the troops. "Make sure they know there's no rest until we finish the job."

Assistant relaxed. *I'm working with a military master.* "Yes, Commander, we'll have four- and five-legged ants back at the front next to their teammates in no time."

Genant turned from side to side and surveyed his ranks. "Okay, Major, we've cut through their senior termite troops. Now let's show them how we really fight." He tapped Assistant on the shoulder. "First, have the front-line attack and the second line spray formic acid in the air over the termites. Then, while they're cowering, have the flanks close ranks and encircle them."

"Yes, this is a strategy they've never seen," concluded Assistant. *I can't wait.* "When surrounded, the termites will panic and break ranks, and they'll be easy pickings." *We'll have termite for dinner.*

"Exactly, and keep corralling them repeatedly until we crush them all," crowed Genant. "I know the enemy has more troops to-hexay, but our superior tactics will dominate them."

"Front line attack!" ordered Major Assistant to his platoon as he spurted a sanguine scent, then he commanded next to the second line. "Sprayers at the ready!" Then he addressed the second to fourth lines, "Third- and fourth-lines split left and right and flank the enemy. Sprayers aim between the flanks. Now spray!" He paused, then continued, "Now flanks collapse! Corral those mite mates and mince some meat." *Our girls can't lose.*

After about forty-five hexutes of repeated corralling and mincing, and with the termites nearly decimated, Genant asked Assistant for a report. "Major, is our job almost done?"

Assistant smiled. "Yes, sir, victory is almost certain. We've already slain Captain Slimite and his Sergeant, and our crack team is hunting down that coward Bitemite." *It won't be long now, I promise.*

"Let me know when Bitemite has fallen, and we'll demand surrender," exulted Genant.

Fifteen hexutes later, Assistant reported an update. "Commander, I got a report that Bitemite bit the dust. He was the last termite standing, or should I say kneeling?" He smiled at his general. "We have decimated over three hundred termite troops. We took no prisoners—no surrender is possible when our girls taste termite hemolymph." He wiped the saliva off his maws. "Do you want to advance on the termites in their nest?" *We'll massacre them all.*

Genant stood tall and issued his last order, discharging a stout stench. "No, send a fly to tell them what transpired here and insist they evacuate the colony, or we will terminate more termites."

"Congratulations, Commander Genant! Once again, you have triumphed." *I knew it all along!*

"You should commend our troops. There are no fiercer insects. As for our opponents, they got what they deserved. Though their name suggests they have might—their fight lacks tactics or bite."

Genant banished the remaining termites, including Dinomite, to the unsheltered lands outside of the colony. Assistant reveled in a job well done and celebrated with Genant the departure of the reviled termites. The termites moved further to the west, far from the burrows and the fungi farms. It was near the edge of the Earth Island but close to another marsh, where they started their own fungi farm. Genant never again trusted any termite. The defeat enraged the termites, still numbering in the thousands, and they vowed to avenge the injustice thrust upon them by evil ants.

Dinomite was so upset about his demotion and ejection from the secret mission that he didn't even try to see Antuna. Even if he wanted to, there was no way he could, as his captain told his sergeant to hold him to the grindstone. His new sergeant canceled his leaves and hexek-ends for the first few hexeks. Dinomite realized that he might have perished along with Bitemite and the other termites that had remained on the mission. He knew that this meant Antuna had saved his life again, but he couldn't embrace feeling grateful because she'd almost killed his new career. His mind-warping program continued, and his mind coach convinced him that Antuna was like every other ant. He told Dinomite she was not trustworthy, and he persuaded him Antuna wanted him to fail as a soldier so that the termite armies would have one less dedicated recruit.

A little later, Dinomite's sergeant approached him and told him a bee messenger was at the front gates with a letter for him. Dino went to meet her with a heavy heart, marching up to the messenger with firm, deliberate steps, uttering his words in a voice he hardly recognized. "Beegan, I don't want you bringing messages here anymore." *Leave me alone!*

"But I thought you'd like to know that Antuna recovered," said Beegan.

Dinomite scowled at Beegan. "I am guessing she was never sick." *I know she's an evil, lying ant.*

There was no pause in her reply. "At least you're still alive. I heard Genant's armies killed every termite on the mission."

Dinomite glared. "I'd rather die than trust a deceitful ant." His hemolymph boiled. *I want nothing to do with her.*

Beegan gasped, panting out her next words, "But Antuna's your friend."

Dinomite leached a venomous vapor, "Tell that lying Antuna that I never want to hear from her again. I only agreed to see you so that I could give you that message." *And my message goes for you as well.*

Beegan was at a loss for words until she found them with a look of sour betrayal. "Dino, what happened to you?"

"My new family here, my real companions, have opened my eyes to how evil ants are. If I had been on the mission, I could have saved my new friends." *I can see myself with four dead ants in my pincers.*

"I doubt it, but I guess there's no convincing you now." Beegan turned away. "I'll tell Antuna what you said."

Dinomite gave Beegan a look, one that she couldn't initially place. It was a glare so distant and cold—nothing she'd ever seen before. Then she realized it was the look conveying the end of a friendship—their friendship.

Beegan reported back to Antuna, and she was heartbroken to lose her close friend and even more devastated she hadn't been there to persuade him to think twice. She realized she could do nothing if he developed such a short fuse and wanted to blow up their friendship, but she respected Dinomite's wishes and took solace, knowing that her actions had saved him.

CHAPTER 5

BOUNTIFUL BRAINS BEGET BRAWN

A recipe for a souffle of advanced aggression:

- *a grain of seasoned obsession*
- *a pinch of fresh egression*
- *with a sprig of ripened oppression*
- *egged on by a tumbler full of progression*
- *stirred with forceful transgression*

AS TIME PASSED, the insects explored the territories beyond the Earth Island, and with insect activity, the lands nearby became more fertile. First, various bushes and smaller fruit and palm trees sprang up. Then when sequoia trees spread there, it became impossible for bees like Beegan and Beebie to know where the Earth Island ended, and Poo-ponic's original landscape began. During this period, both the forests and the colony insects flourished. In particular, the reduced demands of a lower gravity allowed the insects to spend more of their energy on mental rather than physical activities. As a result, the insects became smarter, at least those insect families that valued increased brainpower. The brain gain was especially true for ants, who spouted mottos that permeated the planet. One of the more prolific poets coined the phrases: *Strength of body one does find depends upon the strength of mind;* and *no brain, no gain!*

On the lower gravity Poo-ponic, ants honed their power of telekinesis to move many objects, and the more things they manipulated, the higher their intellect soared. When Antuna reached her twenties, the army drafted her, but soldiers also had time off to pursue other interests, as it was peacetime. Most other female soldiers used their spare time to take classes on battlefield tactics. They hoped to impress their male officers and get promoted as officers themselves. Up to that point, only male ants were officers, despite none of them ever having fought on the front lines.

❊ ❊ ❊

Beegan and Beebie's foraging jobs kept them busy, but Antuna had considerable time off in the afternoons and evenings. Beegan perceived Antuna was wavering about what to do. "Antuna, are you still trying to figure out how to use your spare time?"

Antuna shrugged. "Yes, but it doesn't seem like I have many choices." *I don't know what to do.*

"Why don't you do officer training like the other soldiers?"

Antuna rolled her eyes, exuding a bristly bouquet. "I don't like any of the instructors. Male ants are so lazy, and they only do these courses to show off to the girls." *Please don't mention it to me again.*

Beegan perked up and tried to get Antuna enthused. "But isn't it the only way to get promoted?"

Antuna shriveled and curled herself into a small ball, then replied with very little enthusiasm. "That's what they say, but they've never selected a female soldier as an officer. They just call it officer training to get us to work harder." She rolled herself across the ground. "I will not suck up to the instructors for a promotion that I'll never get." *I'd rather die.*

Beegan sank low to approach Antuna. "I guess being a soldier is not your favorite thing?"

Antuna popped her head out to answer Beegan. "Yes, and I don't need more of it in my spare time." *I'll end up like Dino, shunning all my friends.*

Antuna craved an activity that challenged her brain. She yearned to understand the underpinnings of nature and to use that knowledge to improve insect civilization.

"I know!" exclaimed Beegan after some thought. "I heard that some drones in the ant colony started up a math club, and you should join."

Antuna unraveled herself and stood tall. It piqued her interest. "I never heard that. I know little about math, but it sounds more interesting than soldiering." *I bet it's only a guy thing, but I can show them.*

⁂

Before applying to the math club, Antuna studied as many math problems as she could from whoever would teach her. Antuna even asked Beefirst for help, and the Queen arranged for a top bee mathematician to tutor her. Beeometry was the bee who discovered that hive cells were more robust when built as hexagons rather than traditional circles. Antuna's intellect blossomed under

Beeometry's tutelage, and when she was ready, she approached the ant math club organizers and asked if she could join.

Antuna was a little nervous but determined when addressing the math club president. "Arithant, I have been studying hard, and I want to join your math club." *Bet you never had a member like me.*

Arithant laughed and looked over at the club's membership director, Mathant, who snickered under his breath. "Antuna, don't you realize that this is a male-only club?"

Antuna stood her ground, refusing to take no for an answer. "I assumed it was, but only because females are too busy to take the time to study." *And you are too stuffy to let us in.*

Mathant shot a stinging stink. "No, it's because female ants aren't capable of understanding the complex problems we are solving."

"Why don't you go home and clean your formic acid sprayer and get ready for your next battle," jeered Arithant.

"And take your poo out to the marsh while you're at it." Mathant laughed.

The two math club ants presumed that was all. They were typical male ants who believed a female was only good for soldiering or foraging unless she was a princess seeking a mate. But they had never met a female ant quite like Antuna, and she set out to show them it wasn't just their courage that she could match.

Though fuming inside, on the outside, she was cool as a soaked termite, carefully deciding to challenge the pair. "Okay, math whizzes, I'll go home and tidy my room if either of you can answer the math puzzle that I solved this morning." *I know they'll never get it.*

"No way!" complained Arithant. "How do we know someone else didn't give you the answer?"

"Okay, you pose me a problem too, and if I can't solve it, I'll tidy your rooms as well," Antuna dared. "But if I can solve it, you let me into the club and come and take *my* poo out." *No way I can lose to these bozos.*

"Okay, you're on," agreed Mathant.

"Better get your chalk sharpened and your poo pail ready, girl," said Arithant, tossing a piece of chalk in the air and catching it with his pincers.

Excited by the challenge, Antuna stepped forward and chimed in, "Okay, I'll go first. Answer this: 'A girl ant leaves to visit her queen and her sister on Queen's hexay, and she wants to give them each a cherry. But on the way, she encounters seven webs with the same spider obstructing her passage and demanding half of her cherries to spare her life. Since it was Queen's hexay, the spider felt bad and returned one cherry every time he took some cherries from her. How many cherries did she need to start with to have two cherries at the end?' I'll give you ten hexutes to answer." *I'm sure they'll hate that it's about a girl, a queen, and a sister.*

The two math whizzes thought about it but could not solve the riddle.

After eight hexutes, Arithant beamed, "I got it. It's one hundred and twenty-eight. But, no, wait, it's a trick question. Is the sister supposed to be the sister of the queen or the girl?"

"You got the right idea, Ari," gloated Mathant. "The queen is both the girl's queen and her sister. So, the answer is sixty-four."

"No, you're both wrong," lectured Antuna. "The answer is two." *Was I right or what?*

"Two, no way," they yelled together, pounding their fore-limbs on the table.

Then Antuna pulled out her chalk, scribbled two simple equations on a slate: ½ (2) *and* 2-1+1=2, and explained that each time the spider took one of the two cherries, he gave one back. "It's as simple as 1+1, professors." *Now let me hear your question.*

"Ah yes, I see it now," mused Mathant, falling back into his chair.

"Okay, clever girl," sneered Arithant. "But now you must answer *our* question."

Mathant read the question agreed upon by the two club ants. "Okay, here's a problem that no one in our club has solved. If you can crack it, you're in the club: 'An ant family of four, a queen and a drone, and their boy and girl, had a breakfast of seeds. They ate exactly three seeds, and each ant had a seed. How did they do it?' You have ten hexutes."

Antuna thought a few hexonds and crowed. "That's easy. The drone, the girl, and the boy each ate a seed. Then the queen ate the drone." *I know drones would never think of that.*

After the two math club ants thought about the answer for a few hexonds, they grimaced and then grinned.

"Aaah, that's so gross, but you're right," admitted Mathant.

"That's outstanding," praised Arithant. "I guess you're in the club."

Antuna strolled out of the hall with a prideful smile. "Oh, I live in den 204A, don't forget your poo pails." *And I hope you can survive having a girl in your club.*

※ ※ ※

While ants reveled in learning, the other insects in the colony also valued intelligence and worked hard to keep up with the ants. For example, before Beeometry became a mathematician, she was the Mistress of the 'B50-Too' club, whose members had IQs of fifty or above, more brilliant than most ants.

Her slogan to young bees was: "Learn your one plus ones and two times twos, and some-hexay you can join the B50-Too's."

At Antuna's urging, Beegan and Beebie signed up for the club. However, both were anxious when told they had to have an IQ test before joining.

On the hexay of the quiz, Beebie got upset and refused to go, fretting, "Beegan, I can't do it. You're so smart. I'm sure you'll get in. But I'm too dumb to pass that stupid test." *I know it's hopeless.*

"Beebie, you're as clever as me," reassured Beegan. "You only get flustered sometimes. Come with me and remember the time you helped save Antuna and Dinomite. No dumb bee could have done the things you did."

Beegan knew Beebie was more intelligent than she thought she was. Although she was sometimes impulsive and lacked Beegan's rational, methodical demeanor, she was incredibly observant and forgot nothing she experienced. Although often nervous, her stellar memory equaled her unrestrained enthusiasm.

"I guess you're right, Beegan. And I'm the best waggle dancer on our team." Beebie jumped up and started wiggling. *I'll try my best.*

"Yes, you are." Beegan pointed at the exit. "Now you go, girl."

Beebie was confident in her answers when they took the exam, but became frazzled when waiting for the result. "Beegan, I'm sure you passed. And I did okay, but not good enough," she groaned. *I won't make the grade.*

The tester tallied up the scores and returned to where the

sisters were waiting to ask, "Do you want to get your results separately, or will you hear them together?"

"Oh, we're twins, and we do everything together," answered Beegan automatically, before she considered what the question might mean.

The examiner flapped her wings once and announced, "Beegan, your IQ meets the qualifications. You're in the club. But Beebie, I am sorry, you didn't make the cut-off."

Dejected, Beebie lowered her head and spewed a sour scent. Then, before she flew out, she suddenly turned and grabbed the tablet out of the tester's claws. *Let me see that!*

She scanned it and blurted out, "Forty-nine, just my luck!" But then, as she scrutinized the text, she noticed something. "Wait, look at question five. I'm sure my answer is right, but it's marked wrong." *I know I'm right!*

The official asked to see it again, then looked over at Beebie and said, "You're right. I can't believe I made a mistake. Please accept my apology, and welcome to the club."

"Woo-hoo!" shouted the twin bees as they began a mock waggle dance together.

⁂

Flies had a similar club, called the Fly-High Society, although they did not condone IQs since they believed the tests were culturally biased towards ants and bees. Yet, this was an elite club, which only accepted the brightest flies, not meaning fireflies. Flyhi was the Topper of the Fly-High Society, and when not acting as a messenger, he worked hard to build the club. Many believed Flyhi had an IQ over fifty-five, although he refused to take the inaccurate, ant-devised test.

Calling himself a flyosopher, Flyhi lounged on what

resembled a beanbag chair and sucked on a honey stick. "It's not about your IQ or minding your p's and q's. Flying high is about understanding life and its oh so subtle cues." He immersed himself in an airy aroma.

※ ※ ※

Roaches and beetles were a close-knit group and played and studied together. One of their favorite activities was maze building and running. First, they split themselves into their separate insect family groups, with each species creating an elaborate maze. They then challenged the other group to see who ran faster through the other's maze. Sometimes they even challenged ants, who were happy to play along until it became clear after hexs of training that the roaches and beetles always beat the pants off the ants.

Roachester was a star maze runner in his younger hexays and an even better maze builder as he aged. He strongly supported the event's continuation long after retiring from the sport. Beetlebob had also stopped running mazes but, in the last several hexs, had become one of the best maze designers of all time. Every hex, the roach team with the top maze-winning record, took on the top beetle team for the interspecies maze championship. Roachester came out of retirement one hex to help the team challenging the top beetle team. Beetlebob, who had coached the winning team for the last few hexs, led the beetle team.

Roachester taunted the beetle team when interviewed for the upcoming contest. "Beetlebob and his band of four young beetles have produced many records. But facing us, they'll be coming to a sting fight with venomless hordes."

Beetlebob stood before one of his team's constructions,

diffusing a brilliant bouquet. "My team may be young, but we're not fazed. Check out our structures—you'll be *a-mazed*."

It was a near-even challenge, with the two teams forcing the seventh trial in a best-of-seven event. They even had to build an extra eighth maze each, as the two teams finished tied to the hex-hexond in the seventh run. Yet, Beetlebob's group prevailed in the last race, and throngs of screaming fanatical young female fans swarmed the beetles.

≈ ≈ ≈

Most Poo-ponic worms were very shy and interacted little with the other insects, although they were loyal to other worms and insect friends. If you got into trouble, you could always count on a worm friend to dig you out. For hexs, after the roaches and beetles started their annual maze trials, worms came out to cheer them on. Indeed, there was no roach or beetle maze-building event that the worms were not all over or under. Wormwurst was an enormous fan, both in stature and enthusiasm, and she always made an impression with her presence. There was often a period after these events when the worms disappeared. Most insect families thought they cheered so much at the maze events that it took a toll on them, and the worms needed time to rest afterward. One time, though, a small group of wood-boring beetles, including Beetlebob, followed some worms as they slipped underground after a maze trial.

When he surfaced, Beetlebob exclaimed, "So complex you couldn't believe they were made by a worm, but there are oodles of mazes underground where they squirm."

The worms were playing elaborate maze games underground, with none of the other insects knowing about it. Wormwurst did not race, but she was an assistant coach and helped build the underground mazes. From that point forward, maze competitions became three team events, with beetles, roaches, and worms running each other's mazes. But, of course, the beetles and roaches gave the worms a speed handicap as they moved much slower without legs.

～ ～ ～

Despite losing the earlier banishment battle, the spiders on Pooponic were arrogant and supposed their intellect exceeded that of other creatures. The spiders ignored any signs of increased insect intelligence, assuming the bugs could never surpass their arachnid superiors.

Spifry's mom, Spima, and other spiders would say: "We got more legs, we got more brains, and we got the web."

Spiders attacked insects on their own rather than in groups. Learning from their earlier battles with ants, they waited until the last ant in a line crossed their path before spitting at the straggler. The ants in front did not notice until their next stop that a spider had taken the trailing ant. Spima was a good spitter and caught most of her prey when she was off the web. She was proud that, although small, Spifry was also an excellent spitter. She claimed he got it from her, as Spifry's dad was more of a web sitter. Spiders often caught flying insects in webs, while ants were most often ground spitting targets. Whatever way they did it, spiders were accumulating a disturbing number of kills, enough that ants worried whenever leaving the colony.

～ ～ ～

Termites detested any mental activity aside from their instincts and laughed at the nerdy ants and other bugs they watched from the jungles outside the colony. However, termites, including

Dinomite, never forgave the ants for the battle that banished them from the colony and often ambushed small groups of ants out foraging for food. Although not as clever as ants, they surprised them with more significant numbers and won most small clashes.

Mostmite, promoted to general after Bitemite's demise, explained his strategy, "We do not want an all-out war with ants. So, we'll take out a few at a time till we hear their plaintive rants."

Mostmite invited Dinomite, who worked very hard, to a meeting in his office. "Private Dinomite, I am told by your superiors that you are an excellent soldier."

Dinomite stood at attention and provided a prompt reply. "Yes, sir, I try my best." *And if it means killing ants, no one can beat me.*

"I hear your best is far better than anyone else's. You have twice the number of ant-kills as the others in your unit," praised Mostmite.

Dinomite assumed an at-ease stance. "I work hard." His following words slipped out instinctively, "And I hate ants." *My mental training has worked.*

Mostmite let his gaze travel with a brief look of suspicion. "But don't you have an ant friend?"

His memory dared to betray him and drifted back to the better times when he did not believe his last words, but he whiffed it off. Springing back to attention, Dinomite retorted, "She's not my friend anymore. I recently learned what I always suspected. She lied to me to trick me off the coup mission." *Antuna is dead to me!*

"Ah yes, you can never trust an ant," replied Mostmite, with an affirmed sense of pride.

The tension in Dinomite's back lessened. "That's why I am

so motivated to kill them now. You know what they say, 'she may fool me once as I take the ant's bait, but if she tries to fool me twice, she'll be on my plate.'"

"You've learned well, Private." Mostmite approached Dinomite to add a stripe on his shoulder. "You'll be happy to know that I am promoting you to corporal."

"I appreciate that, sir." Dinomite stood erect. "Does this change my assignments?" *Tell me I get to kill more ants.*

"Yes, I want you leading an ambush team."

Dinomite saluted his General. "Thank you, sir. I'll make you proud." A radiant reek oozed from his scent glands. *Ambushes are my favorite.*

Dinomite continued to be a ruthless ant-killer, and every termite wanted to be on his team. Inspired by his new, mind-warped impression of Antuna, he mastered the art of deceit. He often feigned injury or weakness before turning on any gullible ant that thought he was no threat. Hexths after hexths, small groups of ants left the colony and did not return—victims of Mostmite's band of termite outlaws, often with Dinomite as the leader. The termites attacked any colony insect they could, but found ants the easiest targets. Dinomite always insisted his team target ants. Although it was a continual irritant, ants knew some casualties could occur when foraging and, for a time, tolerated the losses as part of nature.

🐜 🐜 🐜

As the population grew, satellite settlements popped up further and further from the central marsh. The original colony expanded with many burrows constructed, and it became Poo-ponic's capital. Beefirst was still the queen bee, and an aging Genant neared retirement. As colony insects traveled between the capital and the outer settlements or foraged for food, more and more clashes occurred between the colony insects and the termites and spiders in outlying regions. Ants were getting caught and killed at an alarming rate. As a result, both spiders and termites became the objects of ever-advancing strategic plans in insect warfare as the other insects tried to avoid these two predators. From an early age, Beefirst and Genant taught the younger generations of colony insects the *triple-A* defense against their enemies—*be Alert, try to Avoid, and Alight when encountered*. As they got brighter, the colony insects no longer tolerated the intimidation by spiders and termites. Ants had loftier goals—to rise and protect the planet's colonies by annihilating their spider and termite enemies. They knew this goal would take brains, and they strove to strengthen their intellectual acumen. Their feeling was: *we can defeat these morons if we only add more neurons*, and *there'll be no relapses if we increase our synapses*.

~ ~ ~

Antuna had not seen Spifry for quite some time, and she worried about him because of a growing anti-spider sentiment in the colony. So, she met him at their hollowed-out meeting log.

Antuna crept into the dug-out log and spotted him. "Spifry, I am so glad you could make it. Did you have any trouble getting here?" *I hope you were careful.*

Spifry slipped out of the shadows and approached Antuna. "Well, we're in the no-spider zone here. But I've learned to move stealthily."

Antuna wrapped both of her antennae around Spifry's waist, then judged his size in a quick up and down. "Yes, I see you are skinny. What are you eating these hexays?" *I'm worried you're not getting enough.*

Spifry spun around to show off his lean physique. "I'm on a vefab diet."

"Vefab, I've never heard of that." *I can't believe you're on a diet.*

"I was on a vegan diet. It stands for veggies, grains, and nuts. But I couldn't handle all the grains and nuts."

"So, what's vefab?" *I hope it includes meat.*

"I made it up myself. The *V-e* still stands for veggies since I eat seeds, pollen, and fungi. And fab stands for flies and beetles. I eat them when they get caught on my web. I need some meat." Spifry laughed. "I let ants, bees, and termites go out of respect for you, the bee twins, and Dino."

Antuna worried about Spifry's slimness and pressed him. "But I thought the spider army fed you." *And I don't think they're doing very well.*

"I quit the army long ago. It's a volunteer army, so I could leave when I wanted."

"But why would you leave?" Antuna asked. *Why didn't you tell me?* "Didn't they treat you well?"

"Yeah, my mates were great." Spifry then cringed a little. "But I didn't like the exercises."

Antuna shrugged. "Why not?"

Spifry pointed at some sticks on the ground several inches away and prepared to spit. "I was one of the best snipers in my unit, and I loved it when we practiced on sticks and stones. But later, they had us using real insects for practice."

Antuna reeled at killing for sport or practice and just leaving the bodies to rot. "What, you killed insects for fun?" *I hate the military.*

"No, we ate whatever we killed and used any extras to feed the young ones."

Relieved to hear that, she asked, "So, what was the problem?" *I'm okay with that.*

Spifry seeped a suffocating stink. "Well, every time I saw an ant or a termite, I would freeze."

"Freeze?" *For real? I'm shocked.*

"I couldn't spit because I kept seeing you and Dino. And finally, everyone noticed I only spat at beetles and flies."

Antuna's head sank. "That's sweet, but I guess they teased you." *Soldiering isn't his thing either, I guess.*

Spifry nodded. "I kept getting disciplined by my superiors, so I quit."

"So, what have you been doing?"

"I live on my own and tend my webs. I build them close to sequoia trees. That way, I get more beetles and flies that like sap. The ones on strong sap often crash into my web. Guess I'm the justice for FUI," joked Spifry.

Antuna raised her eyebrows. "What's that?" *I don't understand.*

"It's flying under the influence," Spifry elaborated.

"Oh, I get it. Would you say the flies are sad saps?" punned Antuna. "Speaking of sap, I noticed some strong sap near here. Do you want to get some?" *We can celebrate your getting out.*

Spifry pulled out some of his thread. "Sure, I'll spin up a bin, and we can bring it back here."

Antuna discretely blocked the exit from the log. "Okay, you make the bin, and I'll go get it. I don't want you getting caught inside the no-spider zone." *We can't take any chances.*

After their fun visit with the strong sap, Antuna did not see Spifry for another extended period. She didn't want to risk having him come into the colony, and she didn't feel safe leaving it. Antuna continued to fear for Spifry because ants were pushing harder to develop advanced methods to fight spiders. How long would it be before she lost another friend?

Antuna used the math club to challenge her brain and proved herself to be one of the brightest ants in the club. But as she got smarter, she wanted to learn more in other fields. Antuna so respected Beeometry's approach of using mathematical principles to improve the lives of bees that she wished to emulate it. It thrilled Antuna when she learned that the famous botanist Brilliant would give several public lectures about how discoveries in botany and chemistry can help understand nature. She attended the classes, keen to learn about the chemistry of nature and how she could apply the knowledge to improve insect society.

Brilliant was exceptionally intelligent, intensely curious, and determined to understand nature.

Brilliant once declared, "The most beautiful thing is the mysterious—to solve and know it can make you delirious."

He was a brilliant teacher and communicated his knowledge to his students and the general community. His popular public lectures started by discussing plant-plant interactions, and he enthralled his audience as he spoke from over his large gray mandibles. "Plants are deadly assassins, no doubt, and their excretions kill weeds that would else choke them out."

He broached plant-insect interplay at the end of his lecture. "These green hired guns keep their best weapons for insects that strive. Using toxins to cripple us or eat us alive."

Brilliant was a pacifist and studied plants for the joy of understanding the wonders of nature.

His mantra was: "Look deep into nature, both the spirit and letter, and then you will know it all so much better."

Antuna approached Brilliant after one of his talks. "Professor Brilliant, thank you. That was a wonderful lecture." *And I want to learn all I can from you.*

"Well, thank you. And what's your name?"

"It's Antuna, sir."

"Please, call me Brilliant. Oh, I remember you. Weren't you the girl who did the science experiment that kicked off the fungi farm?"

Antuna bowed her head slightly, puffing a padded perfume. "Yes, and my friends helped." *I can't believe he remembered that.*

"I appreciate science projects that benefit the public," noted Brilliant warmly. "That's what I try to encourage with my apprentices."

Antuna stood tall once again. "I agree. That's why I wanted to talk to you. I see how your work can help the insect community, and I'd like to learn from you. Can I volunteer and become one of your trainees?" *Please, please! I'll even take out the trash if you ask.*

Brilliant began packing his things. "That is well and good, but I already have an entire slate of apprentices. And I've never taught a female student before."

Antuna did not want to miss this opportunity and only needed a few more moments to impress Brilliant with her creative imagination and scientific enthusiasm. So, she slipped between Brilliant and his remaining belongings on the desk. "Then I could be your first!" *You're brilliant, and you can't be like the other drones. Please accept me.*

Brilliant steered around Antuna and grabbed his chalk case. "Well, I only take on students that have already studied with established scientists, and I don't think your school science project counts."

Antuna grabbed two chalk erasers off the desk and banged them together to keep Brilliant from leaving. "I beg your pardon, but it wasn't a school assignment! I worked with Queen Beefirst. And I studied mathematics with Beeometry before joining the ant math club." *That must count for something. I hope you can see that.*

Brilliant stepped back to avoid the cloud of chalk dust but stalled his efforts to get away when he heard what she said. He gave her words some thought before saying, "Well, now, that is something. You've joined the math club and trained with the Queen bee and Beeometry."

"Yes, I can bring you reference letters if you like," added Antuna. *I'll get them right away.*

"Beeometry is an amazing mathematician," responded Brilliant. "With those credentials, how could I refuse? Okay, I am giving another public lecture at the same time next hexek. Meet me here, one hexour before the talk, and I'll have some ideas to discuss with you about potential projects."

Antuna handed Brilliant the now clean chalk erasers, bouncing with a thrill she couldn't hide. "Thank you, Professor Brilliant. I'll be here, and you won't regret it." *I knew he was a kindred spirit.*

"Good, and you can explain how a young female like yourself has become so accomplished in the science world. Mathematics, no less. I may have some good ideas for you."

🐜 🐜 🐜

By this time, Brilliant already had a small team of scientific apprentices. Some of his other students were also interested in chemistry applied for the good of insects. But at least one of them wished to apply knowledge for another purpose. When

Antuna joined the team, Brilliant had an apprentice named Antistry. Antistry was clever enough to realize ants could use the lessons that they learned from Brilliant to wage war against their enemies. Antistry once said: "Brilliant may be an *insect* botanist, but with war upon us, I am an *ant* scientist."

Antistry was a runt of an ant, smaller than usual but a genius and Brilliant's top apprentice. When he first studied with Brilliant, Antistry made many important discoveries that benefited insect society. Yet, after losing his father to a termite ambush and a close friend to a spider attack, he became obsessed with ways to wage war against them. In his later research, Antistry discovered that various plants in the jungles produced specific neurotoxins that could paralyze and kill their termite and spider enemies hundreds or thousands at a time.

Antistry voiced his discovery. "We have the ultimate weapons to defeat our foes. What spider or termite can defend against these scientific knows?" Chemical warfare worked best with strategic dispersal methods to avoid harming allies. According to Antistry, "Termite death is ant quell, lest we aim to inflict it well."

On the hexay she met Brilliant, Antuna was so excited she showed up at the lecture hall fifteen hexutes early. She found Brilliant had arrived and had written potential projects for her on a blackboard.

Brilliant perked up when he saw Antuna enter the lecture hall. "Good, Antuna, you are early. I finished writing some potential projects for you. Let me first tell you about our recent findings."

Antuna slipped into a chair at the front of the hall. "Yes, please do. I am interested in all your work." *And I'm so excited.*

"Antuna, I do field research in botany and try to understand the chemistry of how plants cooperate with or hinder each other."

"Plants interact with each other?" Antuna quizzed. *This guy knows so much. I'm overwhelmed.*

"Yes, they either release toxins that kill other competing plants that grow near them or create conditions that help strengthen friendly plants," Brilliant replied.

Antuna leaned in to ask, "Could you give me some examples?" *I'm keen to display my curiosity.*

Brilliant liked this ant-girl. "Yes, of course," he responded. "Some reeds release acids that disintegrate the roots of plants that get too close. And some beans have good bacteria that enhance nitrogen in the soil, which helps beets grow."

"Wow, that is amazing," exclaimed Antuna, excreting an ion-charged incense.

Brilliant continued, "Plants also communicate with us insects."

Antuna peppered Brilliant with another question. "How is that, professor?" *I'm keen to learn from the master.*

"How do you think bees find nectar? The flowers chemically signal to them to come and get it."

Antuna arose and stood closer to Brilliant. "That's true, but why do they do that?" *I expect they want something in return.*

"Because they want the bees to spread their pollen from flower to flower, it's the only way they can mate. After all, they don't have legs, but the males and female plants need to get their stuff together—bees kind of play matchmakers by spreading pollen. Few insects know that, but I'm sure Beeometry does. I am surprised she didn't tell you."

Antuna blushed a little. "We were studying mathematics, not botany. But did you also say plants use chemistry to protect themselves?" *I do my best to divert the topic.*

"Yes, that's what I have been studying recently. Several hexths ago, I found these small white flowers that grow on decaying fallen logs in the forest. Then I noticed termites refused to work on those logs."

"Did you find out why?" asked Antuna.

"It seems the termites who brushed up against the flowers got quite sick. So, the flowers were creating chemicals to keep the termites away so that they wouldn't damage their habitat."

"That is so interesting," expressed Antuna. *I see this guy is a genius.*

"That's not all. I had one of my apprentices, Antistry, isolate the chemical, and he determined it was quite poisonous to termites and ants."

"That is good to know." Antuna smiled. "We should keep away from those flowers."

"Indeed, I also noticed these large crimson flowers with thick spiky stems in meadows," continued Brilliant.

Antuna wrinkled her brow. "Yes, I have seen those many times, but I never knew what they were." *I expect you'll tell me.*

"We call them anti-spider plants because spiders won't go near them. They stay away even though they are strong and tall and would make great scaffolds for their webs."

Antuna jumped in, "Let me guess, the stems are toxic to spiders." *That's my best guess.*

Brilliant spoke now with his eyes open very wide. "Yes, on one plant, a spider was wind blown into the stem and got stuck on the spikes. It wasn't a pretty sight, and the spider had convulsions and died in a matter of hexutes."

"That is amazing. It's smart that the spiders stay away from those plants, and I guess the plants don't like webs," surmised Antuna. *Though, I have no idea what it could be.*

Brilliant brought his forelimbs together to mimic choking something. "No, they don't. The sticky spider strands somehow affect their ability to transport water from their roots. And again, Antistry isolated the poisonous chemical."

"I guess it shows you how much you can learn by observing nature," concluded Antuna. *Nature is so wondrous. I am going to love this experience.*

Brilliant motioned Antuna to go to the blackboard. "Yes, let me show you the projects I am proposing. After the lecture, come to the lab, and I'll introduce you to my other apprentices."

*** *** ***

After a few hexeks in the lab, Antuna got to know the apprentices and learned about their studies. She was impressed by Antistry's early studies that helped create antifungal medications that saved the lives of many colony insects. After getting to know her better, Antistry told Antuna about concentrating the chemical from the white flowers. He explained that he had performed secret tests to determine how deadly the concentrate was on unsuspecting termites when placed on logs that don't have the white flowers. He also described how he discovered the structure of the spider poison. He boasted he synthesized an isomer of the chemical to produce insect-kind's most potent spider neurotoxin. Finally, he told her he planned to do secret field experiments with spiders.

Understanding well what Antistry planned and thinking about Dinomite and Spifry and insects dying for no good reason, an outraged Antuna decided she had to convince him to stop his experiments.

Antuna spun her stool, getting directly in Antistry's face. "Do you understand what your discoveries are capable of?" she said with a breezy bouquet. "You could destroy Poo-ponic as we know it." *And to think how much I respected you.*

"Killing a few nasty spiders and termites will not annihilate the planet," mocked Antistry.

Antuna jumped up from her stool, spraying a prickly perfume. "You don't realize the power this represents and how fragile nature is." *I can't believe you don't see it.*

Antistry pointed directly at Antuna. "Spoken like a true female, and fragility is a weakness that needs to be taught a lesson."

Antuna positioned herself between Antistry and his toxin-filled flasks. "You know I am a soldier-ant when I'm not studying here?" *I could snap you like a twig.*

Antistry squeezed past Antuna, grabbed one flask, and released a rasping reek. "Yes, so why don't you go back to your claw-to-claw combat games and leave the global strategic planning to real scientists."

"And I admired you for your earlier applied research," Antuna spat before storming out.

Antuna warned Brilliant about the dangers of Antistry's discoveries, but by this time, Brilliant was so enamored with his star apprentice he thought Antistry could do no wrong. So instead of acting, he decided that her warning was just academic jealousy that sometimes pops up between competing young scientists.

❦ ❦ ❦

A captivating young ant leader, Malevolant, had ambitions to replace the now ailing Genant. He gave rousing speeches about ant-power and developed a large following with ants who feared spiders and termites. He watched the discoveries of Brilliant and Antistry with great interest as he climbed the political ranks. Major Assistant, who most expected would succeed Genant, perished in a spider attack, and no other military-type had filled the void. The public sentiment at the time favored a charismatic political leader rather than a soldier. Malevolant fit the bill as a captivating orator and a motivating trailblazer. Although not trained as an army officer, Malevolant had the mindset of a military hawk. He ascended to the pinnacle of power on a platform that ants and their allied insects should no longer tolerate the abuses inflicted upon them by termites and spiders.

Malevolant was ruthless, and he saw spiders and termites as dupes in a game he played to gain the power he sought to rule Poo-ponic's capital and its outer settlements. He heightened the colony insects' fears by exaggerating the impact of the termite attacks on them. He inflated the numbers of colony insects tabulated as missing and presumed dead because of termite confrontations. The convention was to rely only on witness-based accounts of insects killed by termites. Malevolant ignored these numbers and made up his own totals. He said to his advisers, "It is not what's right or the truth that matters, but a victory that puts termites in tatters."

He also embellished the estimates of colony insect losses to spider attacks, fudging statistics. He understood that ant brainpower and Antistry's discoveries could overcome the natural order of the food chain or the usual predator versus prey dynamic. Malevolant declared to his insect followers, "For hexennia, spiders have had insects on their plate, and it is time to turn the tables—with six legs topping eight!" With their newfound offensive capabilities, he and Antistry argued that insects no longer needed the *triple-A* defensive system. Malevolant led the battle cries of—*Arachnicide is on our side* and *Extermination to the termite nation*. Malevolant's motto on war and peace was: "Our wars will not slow or have ceases until all spiders and termites rest in pieces."

Most of the ants quickly espoused Malevolant's manifesto, but he needed to work hard to convince other insects in the colony. While humans underestimate insect intelligence on Earth, it was apparent that the increased lifespans on Pooponic skyrocketed insect intellect and their use of physical tools to advance their desires.

※ ※ ※

Gaining confidence after her acceptance into the B50-too club, Beebie, like Antuna, studied in her free time after work. However, unlike Antuna, Beebie studied politics, not science. With Antuna's encouragement, she visited Beefirst to learn more about social integration and inter-insect cooperation. Beegan would have been right by her side, but she developed a mysterious ailment that zapped her energy. Beebie assumed she had an internal inflammatory disorder caused by an infection of *Hepatitis-type bee.*

Beebie stood over Beegan, who lay in bed. "Beegan, I wish you could come with me and study with Beefirst."

Beegan lifted her head and shoulders slowly. "Oh, Beebie, I don't have the strength. It's all I can do to get up in the mornings and do some nectar runs, and by afternoon I'm wiped out."

"It doesn't take that much energy to sit and listen to a brilliant mind." However, the awareness that she had to continue her life goals without her ever-present twin shattered Beebie's world, and she struggled not to let the sorrow change her face.

Beegan flopped back down on the bed. "Please understand how drained I am. And I would die if I passed this disorder on to our queen. So, go by yourself."

Antuna saw Beebie one hexay before she met Beefirst, and she explained Antistry's discoveries to her. "These toxins are so powerful that Malevolant and Antistry could wipe out the whole spider and termite population," she explained.

Beebie perked up. "Oh, Beefirst taught me about this. It's called familic cleansing when one insect family extinguishes another, and that's awful." *I never thought anyone would do it.*

"Yes, and if misused, the toxins might even backfire and kill everyone."

Beebie's face went pale. "Can you join me when I meet with Beefirst this evening? We must warn her about this." *I can't believe this is happening. We must stop it.*

As they entered the Queen's chamber, Beebie spoke first. "Your majesty, I hope you don't mind. I brought my friend Antuna to join us." *I've never had a more urgent need.*

Beefirst jumped up from her throne. "Oh no, I remember Antuna well. She's that firefly of a girl that lit up the entire community with her fungi science experiment."

"You flatter me, Queen," stated Antuna. "If I remember, the whole idea was yours."

"No, Antuna, I had some flowery goals, but you scored the nectar."

Bowing before her queen, Beebie interjected, "Queen, Antuna has some important news about her colleague Antistry that you should hear." *I'm afraid this is not just a friendly visit.*

Antuna described the details of Brilliant's botany studies and Antistry's deadly chemistry experiments.

It quite surprised Beebie when Beefirst asked Antuna, "So what exactly was the structural change in the isomer that makes the spider toxin so virulent?"

Antuna explained its chemistry, with Beefirst probing on every aspect while Beebie sat and watched in amazement.

Beebie jumped up from her seat. "I always knew that you had to follow many details to ensure the safety of our community. But I see now that being a queen is about much more than politics." *Queen, you are impressive. I'm floored.*

Beefirst placed one of her claws on Beebie's shoulder, "Beebie, I hope you learn that there's no more dangerous vice than ignorance. To move forward, we must learn everything we can, regardless of our strengths and weaknesses."

"Your majesty, you are inspiring," added Antuna, imparting a radiant bouquet.

"Stop with the formalities," commanded Beefirst. "I'm only trying my best to keep one step ahead of you two."

Beebie laughed. "But what can we do?" *If anyone can help us, it's you.*

Beefirst frowned before she spoke. "Well, I have spoken to Malevolant two or three times about his ambitions and discovered there's no talking sense to him. Sorry Antuna, but I have to say male ants are a different breed. Many ant species on Earth breed only enough drones for mating, and they die shortly after the deed. I am wondering whether that is not such a bad thing."

Antuna giggled, finding immense relief to share her frustrations with Antistry and Malevolant. "No offense taken, Queen. I've had the same thoughts."

"Is there anything we can do?" Beebie issued a plaintive perfume. *I've never felt so desperate.*

"They have fed us a great lie to see danger where none exists. To mistrust our friends and treat strangers as cysts," declared Beefirst. "There's no convincing Malevolant, so you'll have to go to the public."

"You taught me well about standing up for one's views and the power of peaceful protest," said Beebie. "But how can one small bee convince a bunch of ants and other insects?" *You're telling me I must step up.*

"There's never any guarantee of success," began Beefirst. "But many protests start with one individual, sometimes even with teens or younger ones. You have Miss Firefly here, and I expect she may want to put chemistry to the side for now until this matter is resolved," she surmised.

"Thank you, Queen, we'll try our best," promised Beebie.

CHAPTER 6

NOT ALL IS LOST

What are honor, courage, and the meaning of insect life?

Ne'er lose one's morals, resist instinctive hatred,

and oppose unjust quarrels, from hatch till we are dead.

Secure one's progeny by upholding ontogeny

while wrestling the branches of our phylogeny.

DISILLUSIONED THAT BRILLIANT rejected her warnings about Antistry, Antuna put her lab work aside and helped Beebie organize anti-war resistance. Antuna and Beebie tried hard, but their best efforts failed to stop the steamroller Malevolant and Antistry had set in motion. They organized several protests and drew fair-sized groups of anti-war activists. But when Malevolant gave Antuna extra soldier duties, and Beebie began receiving threats, they realized what they were up against.

Antuna met Beebie after training all morning at the ant

base. "Beebie, they told me I have to do double shifts and sleep in the barracks." *I'm so upset.*

Beebie munched on a pollen ball she had gathered on her last flight. "Can you help on your hexays off?"

"They haven't scheduled me any. I know Antistry and Malevolant had something to do with this. If I refuse or quit, my sergeant said I'd be court-mangled or executed for treason."

Beebie dropped her pollen on the ground. "Executed? Wow, they mean business."

Antuna picked up the pollen and made a face after taking a small bite. "Yes, I am afraid you'll have to do it without me." *I'm so sorry, but I have no choice.*

Beebie grabbed the pollen ball from Antuna and popped the whole thing in her mouth, burped, and spoke again. "Many protestors told me they've received death threats and are dropping out. But I can't quit since this cause is too important."

Antuna looked down, releasing a sour stink. "Beebie, I can't do it anymore. I am just so frustrated. I've pushed for insects to cooperate, but no one is listening. Malevolant has everyone excited, and now I can't even leave my ant training base. I'm a soldier, but I can't wage the war I want to fight." *Please don't hate me.*

Beebie gave Antuna a long tender look. "Antuna, don't worry—I've got this. You have inspired many more insects than you realize, and you and Beefirst have given me a purpose that I craved my entire life." She stood tall and flapped her wings. "Beegan always told me I had more enthusiasm and passion than I knew what to do with. Now I know what it's for." A sunny scent flooded their surroundings.

Antuna raised her head again. "Beebie, if anyone has the drive and ability to stop Malevolant, it's you. I may not fight by your side, but I'll always be with you in spirit."

Antuna did not see Beebie over the next few hexeks while confined to her training base. But she learned Beebie stepped up her efforts and held many rallies, attracting more and more insects. Beebie gave repeated fiery speeches that enthralled the sizable crowds who heard her speak. One could say that her unbridled enthusiasm found the reins that guided both her and her followers along a trail that rivaled Malevolant's aggressive course. Her demonstrations continued, and the marches increased in frequency as they occurred night after night. Beebie was often in the news, espousing her anti-war message, and sometimes there were updates that the protests had become violent. One morning, after Antuna had taken part in a three hexay exercise, she got word that Beegan wanted to meet her. After the training, it was fortunate that Antuna had her first hexay off since she started her double shifts. She immediately sent word that she would meet her the following afternoon.

Beegan pulled herself out of bed when her friend arrived. "Antuna, thanks for coming to see me. Unfortunately, I have some horrible news that I heard from a fly friend of Beebie."

Antuna hugged Beegan and flopped into the nearest chair. "What's happened?" *I fear the worst.*

Beegan sat in the chair next to her. "Two hexays ago, Beebie's protest got very violent, despite her pleas for the demonstrators to remain peaceful."

Antuna stood up and stroked Beegan's back with her antennae. "Did Beebie get hurt?" *I should never have let her do this alone.*

"I don't know. Malevolant's goons swarmed the crowd and rounded up the protesters. Only her fly friend escaped."

Antuna threw her forelimbs in the air. "What happened

to them? Were they arrested? Are they going to trial?" *I can't imagine Malevolant massacring them.*

Beegan slumped deeper into her chair, emitting a frigid fragrance. "No, there's been no word. It's like they disappeared, and no official is talking about it."

Antuna sat again, and a chill ran through her. "That's so scary. Did you talk to the police or go to the courthouse?" *I don't believe it.*

Beegan flopped her head down onto the table next to her. "Yes, I've tried everything. I even talked to Beefirst, and she knows nothing about it."

Straightening, Antuna studied Beegan warily. "I am scared. I know what Malevolant is capable of." *Now, I think he could have killed them.*

Beegan lifted her head, filled with a horror she had never felt before—the realization that they had discussed her sister's death. "Me too. I'm afraid they executed them without a trial. If Beebie's gone, I'll die."

Just as worried as Beegan about her adopted sister, Antuna hugged Beegan, trying to soothe some of her fear. "I can't say the thought hasn't crossed my mind, but we must be strong." *I hope there's some other explanation.*

Several tears escaped Beegan's enormous eyes. "Antuna, I've been so sick of late, and this nightmare has destroyed me. I haven't eaten, slept, or worked, and I'm at my wit's end."

"I know, but we must stay strong for Beebie and never give up hope," urged Antuna, radiating a warming whiff she hoped Beegan would catch.

Despite Beebie's absence, anti-war protests continued, with some chanting: *Where, oh where are our lost insects? Malevolant and Antistry are our prime suspects.* Two hexeks later, a news report stated that authorities discovered a mass multi-insect grave on the far side of the sequoia forest, south of the colony. Evidence showed that Malevolant's crew poisoned all the protestors the night of Beebie's disappearance. The ongoing protests ceased. The news was too much for Beegan, who hadn't eaten or slept since Beebie went missing. When Antuna came calling to console her, she found her lifeless body inside one cell of her hive.

"Oh, Beegan. Oh, Beebie. What will I do without you, my sisters?" After seeing Beefirst's attendants coming to remove Beegan's body, she dashed from the hive. Sure she'd never recover from the despair, the attendants got a wailing whiff as she passed by them.

❀ ❀ ❀

The whole insect community now cowered under Malevolant's control, and he persuaded the colony insects to go to war and amassed a large army of bugs behind him. Hit hard by the loss of Beebie and Beegan, Beefirst also gave in to Malevolant's demands. He organized the ants and other colony insects into an army the likes of which Poo-ponic had never seen. Antistry was instrumental to his plan, so Malevolant promoted him to general of the inter-insect armies, although he micro-managed most strategic operations. Yet Malevolant and Antistry were so much of the same mind that Antistry initiated most of Malevolant's directives even before he issued them.

"Antistry, I want you to arrange for armies of ants and roaches to transport your spider and termite neurotoxins throughout the planet," commanded Malevolant.

"Yes, sir, I have them packed up and ready to go," replied

Antistry. *I am itching to use my discoveries to accomplish our vengeful goals.*

Malevolant crossed the room and stood before a large map on the wall. "And have worms dig large tunnels to hide reserves of the chemicals throughout the land."

Antistry approached Malevolant and touched various sites on the map. "The worms are ready, and we identified many caves we can use as transportation hubs." *We're prepared.*

Malevolant extended his forelimbs. "Excellent. Also, have wood-boring beetles drill holes in dead and alive trees everywhere. Then our ant soldiers can fill the holes with formic acid or the termite toxin."

"Yes, the ants will use telepathy to spread the poisons," explained Antistry. "The formic acid will kill on contact, and the toxins will seep into the wood the termites eat." *I can fully imagine the suffering we can inflict on our hated enemy.*

Malevolant rubbed four claws together. "Perfect, and the termites are too stupid to realize that the boreholes are a trap, and they won't know we poisoned the wood until they've eaten it. By then, it'll be too late." He then stood erect and proclaimed, "What luck for us insects who link that these termites don't plan or think."

Antistry smiled. "Yes, Malevolant, this will be an easy victory against the termites." *I am ecstatic I can finally avenge my father's murder at the claws of evil termites.*

"As for the spiders, you should have bees and flies perform flying raids to drop water bombs filled with neurotoxins over spider webs," advised Malevolant.

Antistry looked out the Malevolant's office window. *Our offensive is a tribute to my lost friend.* "The spiders will not differentiate the toxins from rain or fallen dew, and the poison will paralyze them before they know what they have crawled into." A sour stench polluted the air.

❋ ❋ ❋

Spiders fought back and quadrupled their normal web-building activities, bearing their fangs often as they caught more insect prey. Flies and bees caught in webs as they flew back to the colony were stung and ripped apart by the spiders' sharp fangs as they struggled to free themselves. As they scurried back from setting their traps, individual ants, roaches, and beetles were ensnared and corroded by the spiders' burning spit. The sticky silk paralyzed their writhes and burned through their exoskeletons, causing searing pain. Spifry had already quit the army and laid low, hoping to evade the draft back into service.

Throngs of termites also swarmed worms as they set out to dig ammunition tunnels. The termites eviscerated the worms who were too slow to escape, eating them from the inside out as they strove to tunnel their way to safety underground. Dinomite fought hard for his termite mates but preferred to attack ants rather than worms. Despite the minor victories for spiders and termites, the more ingenious colony insects determined ways to limit detection and spread the toxins throughout the planet.

❋ ❋ ❋

The still-grieving Antuna rejoined her army unit, but not because she wanted to fight. She had ulterior motives—to find Dinomite and Spifry. She hoped to convince them to escape to the far side of the planet or the outer settlements where the fighting had not reached. Beefirst sent her a message of condolence on the bee sisters' deaths. She told Antuna she endeavored to convince

Malevolant to allow a small group of termites and spiders to live near the outer settlements if they promised to leave the colonists alone. Antuna didn't know if Malevolant would accept Beefirst's proposal, but Dinomite and Spifry might survive if he did. Antuna replied to Beefirst, asking about Malevolant's decision. If he agreed, she planned to bring Dinomite and Spifry there to live.

It pleased Antuna to learn that her next mission would take her to an area with a lot of dead wood she expected Dinomite was guarding. Dinomite hid in the shadows when he saw the ants approaching with the beetles following. Antuna was with a small group of four ants, and Dinomite's group comprised seven termites, including himself. The other termites jumped them when the ants passed, and the beetles scattered. Dinomite held back at first, playing his signature lame termite trick, whereby he lay still until he pounced on any ants remaining who thought they were victorious. Antuna was at the back of the pack, so she dodged the initial melee when the other ants and termites had seemingly killed each other. Antuna was the only one standing when Dinomite sprung on her. She realized it was Dinomite when he lunged, and she fired her deadly acid spray far off to his left. Dinomite didn't know it was Antuna until he pinned her and prepared to bite off her head.

Antuna screeched, "Dino, it's me, Tune!" *Don't hurt me.*

Dinomite heard her, and his mind raced while he waffled between thoughts of hatred and friendship. The same battle he'd been fighting for longer than he'd ever wanted. In the end, he spared her life but accused her, "I hate you. You got me demoted and reassigned from my unit. You are a lying, evil ant, like the others."

Antuna relaxed, despite still being in Dinomite's clutches. "I saved your life." *Were my motives lost on you?*

Dinomite loosened his grip but remained on top of her. "You were never sick."

Antuna stroked Dinomite's face with her antennae. "No, but I knew you'd die. So, I wanted you to abandon the mission. It was the only way." *If he only knew how much I cherish him.*

Dinomite's hatred of Antuna waned the more time he spent with her, as Antuna exhibited the same gentleness and caring she always had, forcing him to recognize it.

Dinomite leaned back but stayed within Antuna's antennae reach. "Well, it worked, but my career suffered, and I was a laughing stock."

Antuna caressed Dinomite with her forelimbs and spoke with a fragile fragrance. "But you're alive, and I want you to stay that way. Promise me you'll flee to the outer settlements. There's a chance that some termites and spiders can live there in peace." *And perhaps we can rekindle our friendship.*

Dinomite got up but still stood over Antuna. "What, desert and abandon my mite-mates? I can't do that."

Right then, one of the fatally injured ants turned and saw a termite standing over Antuna and blasted his formic acid all over Dinomite before collapsing again. Dinomite buckled back in agony as his exoskeleton burned, and he slowly succumbed to his injuries. Antuna grabbed onto Dino and held him even tighter than she had when he slipped underwater in the marsh. Dino gazed upon her with a mournful look that conveyed his sorrow for the time they had lost. In the hexutes before he died, he described to her his mental training and the interactions he had with his superiors, his new friends, and Mostmite. When he realized the end was near, he tried to justify his actions and atone for the horrible way he had treated Antuna, either overtly or in his mind.

Before Dino died, Antuna stroked him with the gentleness of a mother caressing a newborn child. "I've never considered you as anything but a friend, and I forgive you for your hateful thoughts and deeds." *It is all behind us.*

Dinomite relayed one last line to Antuna before he died, "Put me back in the water, Tune, I'm burning up."

As he died, everything inside her broke, and she cried out, "I am so sorry, Dino. I tried to save you once more, but you spared me. I hope in our next life, wars don't exist, and we can be friends forever." *I only wish Beefirst had gotten her way.*

Unfortunately, the war continued. The increased spider web construction and occasional termite ambuscades were no match for the organization and cunning of Malevolant's superior insect armies. Antistry's toxins paralyzed and smothered hundreds of thousands of spiders each morning as they traversed their dewy webs. The neurotoxins worked on contact and were absorbed through the spider's hairy skin. It was painless at first but later caused each spider's nerve endings to explode with noxious shooting impulses as they gasped for breath. The spiders drowned in a sea of air that they could not inhale with their immobilized tracheae and book lungs.

In keeping with Malevolant's plans, millions of termites died, too. They were liquified as they entered booby-trapped boreholes or poisoned as they gnawed through deadwood for food or shelter. If they entered a laced borehole, the acids melted them as they slipped into the depths. If a termite ate contaminated wood, it died an agonizing death when its stomach ulcerated as the lining slowly dissolved. The contents leaching out caused long-lasting smoldering pain and an escalating, life-ending fever. Malevolant's armies utterly demoralized the spiders and termites with all the pain and suffering, and only a few thousand stragglers hid where they could.

In a fiery speech designed to inspire a final push by his troops, Malevolant summarized the effectiveness of the intelligent teamwork used to defeat the termites and spiders, "What termite can muster a surprise ambush when our embedded fever knocks him on his tush?" He continued, "An insect brain-gang is mightier than the spider's twain-fang!"

As the war neared its conclusion, Antuna received an extended leave. She spent her spare time searching for Spifry and found him hiding in the hollowed-out log where they had last met. Antuna had a feeling that he might be there. Still, before she saw him, she received a message from Beefirst, who told her that Malevolant consented to allow the remaining holed-up termites and spiders to live near the outer settlements.

Antuna ran up to Spifry and hugged him. "Fry, somehow I knew I'd find you here. Did you hear about Dinomite, Beegan, and Beebie?" *I am sure you have.*

Spifry slumped a little in Antuna's embrace. "I came here to say my goodbyes. I expected you would come too."

They shared a long hug to comfort each other in their collective grief. Although not as close to the bee sisters and Dino as Tune was, Spifry fondly remembered the good times with his childhood friends, and it saddened him to know that these youthful memories would be all he had left of those that cared most about him. But he held onto the fact that he still had Antuna, the anchor that had moored them all together.

Antuna crawled over to the opening of the log. "Let's give a toast to our old friends. I saw some strong sap pooled up on top of the log. Do you want some?" *They deserve our praise.*

"Well, if it's a tribute to Dinomite and the bee girls, I can't refuse," buoyed Spifry.

Antuna and Spifry scooped out the strong sap, and after an initial long, shared cry, they had a downright giddy time saluting their old friends and reminiscing about the old hexays.

After they finished the last of the strong sap, Antuna declared, "Spifry, I'm quitting the army, and I want to take you to the outer settlements." *I don't care what Malevolant thinks.*

Spifry jumped up. "Whatever for? You'll be risking your life harboring a fugitive."

Antuna frowned and leached a rutted reek. "I tried to convince Dinomite to come when we met in battle. But my troop-mate sprayed him right before me, and he died in my embrace, a victim of this awful war. I don't want that to happen to you." *You are the last of my best friends.*

"We may get caught, and they'll kill us both!" exclaimed Spifry.

Antuna straightened herself. "We can travel at night and hide in the shadows in the hexay. You've been able to avoid detection." *We can do it together.*

"I survived because I don't build webs anymore and eat only fruit and seeds," explained Spifry.

"So, you can show me how to avoid capture. As a deserter, I'll be a fugitive too." *It'll be an adventure for us.*

Spifry frowned. "But why do you want to travel to the outer settlements? What's there?"

Antuna spread her forelimbs wide. "Amnesty! Beefirst told me that Malevolant has agreed to let some termites and spiders live in the territories next to the outer settlements." *We have to try.*

"And you believe the promise he gave to Beefirst?" asked Spifry.

"I trust Beefirst, but not Malevolant," responded Antuna. "That's why we should escape and wait until we find out whether it's a trap." *It's our only hope.*

Spifry had been so secluded since the spider banishment that he felt like a hermit losing his mind. He approached Antuna for another hug, streaming a syrupy scent. "To tell you the truth, Tune, I've been so lonely. I'd follow you anywhere."

"Okay, let's sleep off this strong sap and leave when it gets dark," concluded Antuna.

The voyage to the outer settlement was not very far, but troops were on the move everywhere, and they took care to avoid detection. Most of the armies redeployed during the hexay and slept at night. The two needed to find safe hiding places during the hexay and were careful not to disturb any slumbering troops as they traveled at night. Luckily, the war was culminating, and there were not that many skirmishes. The few units they passed didn't even have sentries stationed on a watch. As Spifry had been avoiding detection for hexs, he was a master at stealth and taught Antuna what he knew. They lived off fruits and seeds, which gave them more than enough to eat and drink, with the latter supplemented by the morning dew.

When they reached the outer settlements, Spifry hid while Antuna searched for accommodations. Antuna explained to the manager of the burrow that her settlement had failed, and she sought another one. Things like that often happened in the new territories, so the administrator was not suspicious. Antuna also told the manager that her superiors relieved her from duty as she injured her back helping the war effort. The outer settlements were still young, and the officials tried hard to attract new settlers. It was a rough and tumble area, like the American wild west in the late 19th century. There were many deserters and vagabonds in the outer settlements, and nobody asked questions. The attitude was: so long as you can take care of yourself—go for it. The bonus was that the nest rooms were larger, since the burrows were far from full. Thus, there was plenty of space to hide Spifry until they could learn whether Malevolant's amnesty offer was legitimate.

As the hexeks passed, troop movements continued, and Malevolant transported termites and spiders to the area as prisoners. Some also came on their own. They lived in zones outside the settlements the ants called reservations. Over the hexths, the reservations filled up, but Spifry stayed in the burrow with Antuna because they enjoyed each other's company and excelled at hiding Spifry from detection. With the reservations filled, Antuna discretely sought other ants, bees, and beetles that might consider hiding termites and spiders. Before long, she became the covert leader of the insect underground trailway. Antuna and her network of sympathetic insects saved thousands of termites and spiders, at least for a period. Antuna learned all about the current war and the earlier banishment battles from her compatriot ants and the rescued termites and spiders.

One quiet evening, while dining with Spifry, Antuna said, "I am so glad that you agreed to come here with me." *I may have lost a lot, but I still have you.*

Spifry spat out the shell of a seed he swallowed. "Me too. It was I hide here or there, but now I have company. And I am so proud of you for your efforts to save so many termites and spiders. The underground trailway has been an amazing success. I'm sure Dino is looking down at you and smiling."

Antuna grabbed another seed and husked it for Spifry. "I've been thinking a lot about Dino, and especially Beegan and Beebie, lately." *I can see life is so fragile, and for what?*

"Yeah, I miss them too," declared Spifry.

Antuna popped a seed into her mouth. "No, that's not what I mean. It's more like—is that all there is? We live for a while, and we die, and it seems so pointless." *I want more.*

Spifry grabbed a few more seeds. "Well, you help the colony survive. And your queen has babies, so the colony lives on."

Antuna smashed one seed on the table. "That seems so inadequate. I wish ants were more like spiders, and any female could have babies." *I so wish I could be a mother.*

Spifry brushed the shell off the table and pushed the seed meal towards Antuna. "They don't all have babies, only the strong ones."

Antuna sighed. "Yes, but it's not predetermined at birth." *Why can't I have a family?*

Spifry husked a seed for himself. "Well, accept it, Tune, you're not a spider. You are what you are."

Antuna glared back at Spifry, oozing an achy aroma. "What am I if I can't have babies and pass on my genes?" *My line will end!*

Spifry gave Antuna a loving look, as if he had prepared to answer the question his entire life. "You're a brilliant ant and a great friend."

"Thanks for that. But can I tell you a story about my early life on Earth?" asked Antuna.

"Sure Tune, I got nowhere to go," Spifry admitted.

Antuna laughed. "You can say that again."

Spifry smiled. "I got nowhere to go!"

"Stop kidding. I'm serious," Antuna protested. *Doesn't he realize how much this means to me?*

"Okay. Tell me," urged Spifry.

Antuna leaned in closer. "When I was young, my mother, our queen, called me her little princess." *And I think I know why.*

"Doesn't a mother always call her girl a little princess?" queried Spifry.

Antuna leaned back again. "Not with ants. You're a princess or not, and to call someone a princess when they are not would be hurtful." *I think I was her princess.*

Spifry frowned. "So, why did she call you a princess when you ended up being a soldier?"

"I never knew. I expect I was meant to be a princess, but somehow didn't make the grade or something," surmised Antuna. *So, they bumped me out.*

"Really?"

Antuna leaned in closer to Spifry again. "Yes, I remember one hexay when my mother said, 'You're growing up now, and I can't call you my little princess anymore.'" A single tear dropped from her left eye. *I've never felt so devastated.*

"Oh, is there more?" Spifry questioned.

Antuna continued, "Then she gently bit off my wings. Although I was small compared to my sisters, she said I was such a fighter, I would likely be a soldier when I grew up."

Antuna struggled to keep her upper lip from quivering.

Somehow, she'd avoided the memory, but now that she'd said it aloud, there was no burying the emotions that followed.

Spifry put the remaining seeds away. "That must have been quite the upsetting hexay."

Antuna lowered her head. "Yes, and later that night, she told me I had to move to another part of the hive. She told me to say goodbye to my sisters, and I cried and asked why I had to go. She said they would take extra special care of me and groom me to be a soldier or a worker." *I was a wreck.*

Spifry rubbed Antuna's shoulder. "Ouch, that must have been tough."

"Yes, and I noticed two funny things." Antuna started again. "First, they didn't feed me as much." *Some extra special care! I felt abandoned.*

"And what was the second?"

Antuna looked down at her belly. "I noticed that none of the other girls there had pouches." *They tossed me in with the sterilized ants.*

Spifry looked at Antuna all over. "Pouches, what do you mean?"

Antuna rolled over to show her abdomen. "Pouches, like this one here. Although mine has shrunk a little." *A pouch I could never use.*

"Is that where ants store their unfertilized eggs?" asked Spifry.

Antuna laughed. "Yes, and Antistry said spiders were stupid." *I expect you know what I'm getting at.*

Spifry stood up from the table. "Are you thinking that you might have babies now? That's crazy."

Antuna explained to Spifry how she learned from Beeometry that ants and bees are very similar and that only the princesses that get a lot of food become queens. Both eat lots of sugars and proteins, which help their eggs develop. Although princess bees get their nutrients from royal jelly, which worker bees excrete from glands in their heads, ant princesses just need to eat a lot of sucrose and protein. Then she said Brilliant taught her that honeydew tasted so sugary-good because the aphids that expel it bite right into the part of the plant that produces sucrose. He also told her flower's phloem sap is packed with proteins.

"Since there are no aphids around, to nourish my eggs, I need to suck sucrose and proteins from plant phloem sacs as aphids do," Antuna said. *I wonder if it's even possible now.*

Spifry raised his pedipalps. "Isn't this stuff moot? Even if you stimulate egg production, don't you need a drone to fertilize the eggs?"

"Yes, and..." Antuna started.

Spifry rubbernecked towards Antuna. "What?"

Antuna blushed and turned toward the doorway. "I bumped into a drone yester-hexay that I remember from the math club back at the colony. He was smart, good-looking, not a jerk like most others, and liked me." *I think I'm going to sob.* "But what if my eggs are dried up?"

"The way you're talking, it sounds like you're having a surge," exclaimed Spifry.

Antuna stared intently at Spifry. "A surge. What's that?" *Please tell me this is a good thing.*

"Well, in the spider family, sometimes older mothers get a surge. So, they produce eggs late in life when everyone says they're too old. By the way, what's the drone's name?" Spifry asked.

Antuna laughed out loud. "You will not believe me. His name is Surgeant." *I kid you not.*

"Did you say Sergeant or Surge-ant?" asked Spifry.

Antuna laughed some more. "His name is Surge-ant." *Believe me. What are the odds?*

Spifry jumped up and patted Antuna on the back. "Sounds providential to me."

Antuna laughed some more. "Yes, where's the nearest phloem sac?"

Antuna spent the next few hexths draining sucrose and protein from every flowering plant she could find. Spifry complimented her on how shapely and full-figured she had become.

Antuna waddled over to Spifry one afternoon. "Do you think I'm ready, Spifry?"

"I'd say you were a PALM, girl," laughed Spifry.

Antuna stared hard at Spifry. "What's that?" *He must be kidding me.*

Spifry laughed again. "A Princess Ants Like to Mate."

Antuna headed towards the doorway. "Hah, that's a good one. Okay, I gotta go find my Surge drone."

❈ ❈ ❈

It did not take long for Antuna to find Surgeant. He had noticed her physical changes and hung around the neighborhood, waiting to meet her. When he saw her that evening, he came right up to her and said, "Tune, you're looking good these hexays. Did you go on a diet?"

Antuna blinked her eyes repeatedly, secreting a sultry scent. "Yes, I am glad you noticed." *This is my chance!*

Surgeant opened his eyes wide. "How could I not? You're *gorge-ous.*"

Unlike humans, ants are not shy about these encounters and waste little time talking.

"I don't have any wings, though. Have you done this before, Surge? I never..."

Surgeant picked up Antuna without answering, and they

flew off together into the sunset. The date was a success, and Antuna laid her fertilized eggs in the larvae section of a fungi farm on the edge of the settlement. She thought to herself, *with the war ending, my children, your opportunities will be endless. Grab on to life and never let go.*

When she got back to her nest, Antuna told Spifry about laying the eggs and how she worried about how they would do. "I can't raise a family here, so they will have to go it alone." *But at least my line will continue.*

"Sorry if concealing me is getting in the way," Spifry apologized.

Antuna shrugged her shoulders. "No, it's the war and me deserting. I don't want to attract attention, and I only need one or two to survive to make it worthwhile." *I believe it will work.*

"I am sure they'll be fine, and some hexay, you'll have lots of little grand-ants," Spifry consoled.

Antuna stared back towards the fungi farm and sighed.

Over the next few hexeks, Antuna spent her spare time visiting the fungi farm to check on the eggs and later the hatched larvae, which appeared to be thriving. She was comforted knowing that her babies didn't have predators in the settlement with the spiders on the reservation. One hexay, when Antuna returned to the burrow, a fly waited for her outside. As he was a royal envoy sent by Beefirst, she was excited until she received the message and detected its bitter bouquet.

She entered the nest and told Spifry about the dispatch. "Fry, I got a letter from Beefirst, and she said Malevolant poisoned every spider and termite on the reservation." *That scoundrel. I've never hated anyone so much.*

Spifry stamped his eight legs in frustration. "That's horrible. He went back on his promise!"

Antuna looked over both her shoulders. "She also said that Malevolant found out about the underground trailway. He has instructed the ant armies to inspect the burrows for fugitives, and they're executing everyone." *He won't stop at anything. I'm not surprised.*

Spifry's following words came out heavy. "All the fugitives?"

"Yes, and those that harbor them, after public shaming," responded Antuna. "Luckily, they don't know who the leaders are." *We might be safe.*

Spifry paced back and forth like a caged animal, spraying a smothering scent. "I thought it would come to this, but I hoped we'd have more time."

Antuna stepped into Spifry's path to stop him from pacing. "Fry, we have to double our efforts to keep our secret. First, I'll have to warn all the others, and they can't find out you are here!" *Our lives depend on it.*

"Okay, you have permission to kick me if I snore," Spifry joked.

Antuna gave him one of her looks. "I'm serious, Fry. This is life or death!" *I know he's joking just to make me feel better.*

Spifry stopped pacing and headed toward the exit. "I know, Tune, but what more can we do? I've lived like a hermit crab hiding in a shell for hexths. You can live in peace if I leave."

Antuna blocked the doorway. "No, I would die knowing that they captured and killed you because I couldn't protect you." *We're in this together!* "So, we must be extra careful. Never go near the doorway and walk super softly."

Spifry mimicked a walk. "Like a spider?"

Antuna smiled. "Yes, like a stealthy spider." She looked

hard at Spifry as if she wanted to memorize his face—or rather this moment—before turning toward the fungi farm.

~ ~ ~

Spifry was extra careful, and hexeks passed with no hint that others knew he was there. Antuna repeatedly visited her larvae, who metamorphosed into pupae and then into nanitics. Each hexay she visited, she imparted her life and friends' complete story. She described the struggles and delights on the new planet and insisted they pass the stories on to their offspring.

Antuna told them about how Beegan, Beebie, and Spifry had saved her life and how they saved Dinomite's life. She described how Beefirst wanted all insects to work together. Antuna told her children that as their lives were longer than their ancestors on Earth, they could learn much more and do things differently. She shared how she had been a community activist, a soldier, a resistance leader, and a scholar, and she described the outstanding teachers she had. And she told them she was a mother, even though she wasn't a queen.

"You are the future," she sprinkled a pointed perfume, "but you are also the window to the past. Strive to help others, have your own families, and ensure these stories forever last."

~ ~ ~

As she returned from another visit, she heard the loud commotion of a growing horde of ants lining the two sides of a wide path near the outer settlement's central square. The mob got louder, calling out: "There they are!" and shouting: "Traitors, kill them both!" as they stared at a procession moving down the road. She squeezed through the maze of ant limbs to look at what they watched.

Antuna trembled as she later described the scene with a blistering bouquet. "Fry, it was horrific. Everyone shouted and threw stones at the poor spider and the ant. The sheriff and his deputies whipped the spider whose hemolymph soaked the path as they made him march by the crowd. They must have had him spit at the ant, forcing him to drag her behind him. The stones hitting her and the ones he dragged her over made her exoskeleton peel off." *Discussing this is making me feel ill.*

Spifry shuffled closer to her, hiding his own horrified expression. "Tune, I am so sorry you had to see that. Try to erase it from your mind. They'll never discover us—we've been so careful."

Without acknowledging Spifry's comment, she shook like a leaf in a windstorm. "When they got to the central square, they used the spider's thread to tie them to the old sequoia marked for the beetles to take down. The sheriff sprinkled a silver powder over them and told the crowd to spray them down with their formic acid and move back fast." She stopped and listened for a short time at the door. "The spider and ant strewed a pealing perfume when the formic acid hit their tattered skin. Then, in a matter of hexonds, there was a deafening explosion, and they both burst into flames." *It's the most horrific thing I've ever seen.*

"I can't believe it. The mob burned them alive!" declared a shocked Spifry.

"Yes, in an instant, they were gone. Even the old sequoia burned to ashes in hexonds. It was horrendous—I can't forget the piercing screech before the fireball. It was like the two were the tree limb that attracted a blazing lightning bolt." Antuna gasped out her last description before collapsing to the floor.

Spifry picked her up and held her close, but didn't know what to say to allay her fears.

Antuna shuddered as she spoke. "Fry, I ... I ... I can't go like that. Promise me if they come here, you'll take me out first." *He must, or I will.*

Spifry backed away from her. "No, Tune, I can't do that."

Antuna crawled forward and got into Spifry's face. "You must promise, or I'll kill myself right now."

Antuna sensed Spifry wanted to slap some sense into her, but she realized he could never hit her. "Okay, but let's not dwell on it for now," he stammered.

"Yes, Fry, let's cherish the time we have left," Antuna murmured. *Why can't we all live together in peace?*

❈ ❈ ❈

A short while later, Antuna returned to visit her children but discovered most of them had left the marsh and made their way into the world.

She spoke to one that remained at the marsh. "I fear that my time on this planet is running short. I once said we would all die if insect families could not let go of old grudges. Our failure to unify has taken the lives of my three closest friends, and Spifry and I may soon join them." *I fear that time is very near.*

Her child asked, "But you told us of all the great things you and your friends did to bring insects together. Has this not helped?"

"Sometimes lessons are learned only after great tragedies, and when the teachers are but ghosts that come to us in our pheromonic dreams. In my visions, I have seen this war is only a prelude to greater catastrophes that will befall our planet unless we learn to cooperate." *Don't ever forget what I have told you and pass it on to your heirs.*

Her child replied, "So we must continue to convince all families to work together?"

"Yes, and I dreamed of a time after a great upheaval when our families join. But my vision showed me our world will not thrive until the wise listen to the naïve, and the strongest among us depends upon the meekest."

※ ※ ※

Although Antuna told Spifry that she never wanted to discuss the shaming and burning incident again, she could not forget the images she saw. She kept reliving the incineration in her dreams and tried to understand how such a fire could ignite so quickly.

After hexays of brooding, she finally brought it up with Spifry at dinner. "I can't stop thinking about the fire. What could burn that hot?" *I know it's not possible without some trick.*

Spifry looked up at her over his bowl of berries. "Tune, forget about it. It's likely some new nasty invention of the evil chemist Antistry."

Antuna grabbed one berry and skewered it violently with her pincers. "Oh, by the death of my queen, you're right! After leaving the lab, I heard Antistry experimented with chemicals like sodium and potassium to make a flamethrower out of ants' formic acid spray. He gave up because of backfires that were injuring too many ants. I know formic acid is explosive when mixed with sodium or potassium." She peppered Spifry with a popping perfume. "It produces volatile hydrogen gas that explodes. That evil Antistry. He finally found a wicked use for his idea." *I can't believe it.*

Spifry shook his head. "Okay, Tune, you figured it out. Now let's try to forget about it and live like normal fugitives."

"Haha, like normal fugitives—that's funny! I'll do my best," said Antuna.

∼ ∼ ∼

A few hexths later, they heard shouting at the entrance to their nest, and the two friends sensed the patter of many six-legged footsteps heading toward Antuna's den. Spifry grabbed Antuna and held her close as she shivered. Their hug lasted only hexonds, but it seemed like hexours. Antuna relaxed in his gentle embrace.

Spifry whispered, "Should we try to run, Tune?"

Antuna quivered hard. "No, they'll catch us and burn us." She lowered her head. *We must do it now.*

Spifry held her tight in response. "I guess this is it, Tune. I'll make it quick."

Antuna closed her eyes and dispersed a feathery fragrance. "Yes, Fry, I'm ready. It's been a good life." *And I'm happy we'll go together.*

Spifry squeezed Antuna a little tighter, like how a mother spider hugs her young before they leave the nest. "I know, and I couldn't have picked a better soul to resuscitate and befriend."

Antuna rocked herself into a trance. Spifry barely heard her withered whiff. "Ouch, did you just bite me, Fry?"

Spifry crawled across the den, and before he drank from the flask that Antuna had filled with formic acid and poppy juice, he said, "Goodbye Tune, my first bite gave you life—and now with my last, it ends. But, girl, we had some good kicks."

In the hexonds, before the poison took hold, Spifry pulled out his thread and wrapped Antuna and himself into a tight cocoon. They planned to leave their world bound in death, like their long friendship.

※ ※ ※

Malevolant's fugitive-hunting squads found the cocoon and planned to burn their bodies after cutting them out. However, one ant recognized Antuna and pleaded that they bury her instead. Antuna had become a folk hero with the stories of her resurrection, fungi farm building, gender role reversals, war resistance, and miraculous motherhood. Although the soldiers typically followed Malevolant's orders to the chemical formula, they made an exception in her case. The soldier that knew her learned she had offspring and took her body and Spifry's to her young nanitics. She helped Antuna's children bury them under a maple tree close to the fungi farm at the marsh where they hatched.

Malevolant and his armies were content. The ants, bees, flies, roaches, beetles, and worms were finally rid of their enemies. Had Antuna not ensured her progeny, future generations would not have known how insects arrived, survived, and prospered on the new planet and how termites and spiders met their end. In the hexuries after the war had ended, growing numbers of colony insects learned of Malevolant's various deceptions and regretted their horrific treatment of termites and spiders.

In time, Antuna's grave became a shrine. There was a rekindled sentiment that colony insects should strive to live peacefully together, as Antuna and her friends had encouraged. Antuna's story became a folktale that every colony insect learned from her direct descendants, who became revered in society as Antunites or the keepers of Antuna's story. The colony insects lived in peace for many mega-hexs until another evil leader reignited hatred in his quest for power.

CLOSING PODCAST [INTERVIEW]

Vive: As promised, I'm joined by our interstellar author, Narrant from moon Bilaluna, of our sister planet Poo-ponic. Now that we have finished Volume 1 of the history, we will discuss it with Narrant. Welcome back, professor.

Narrant: Please call me Narrant. I don't even own a lab coat.

Vive: Poor Antuna and her friends went through a lot. They learned so much, and then things went sour.

Narrant: My ancestors lived much longer on Poo-ponic than insects on Earth, and they got much brighter. [00:31] But intelligence is not the same as wisdom, and instincts are hard to overcome.

Vive: Right, we humans can relate to your story. We did things to other cultures and species throughout our history of which we are not proud.

Narrant: Yes, we too have had our dark times, as you have heard.

Vive: Narrant, would you field some questions from our audience?

Narrant: Yes, of course.

Vive: Joe asks: "What were the psychological effects of such a traumatic experience with the Great Displacement? How did the insects cope on a mental level?" [01:00]

Narrant: Well, Joe, insects are very adaptable creatures. And the Cretaceous period on Earth was a dangerous era, so moving to a planet with few predators was less stressful for many of them.

Vive: Change can sometimes be good, allowing insects to evolve.

Narrant: But as your history tells you, societies can sometimes go through troubles of their own making. On Poo-ponic, things seemed fine, and quite suddenly, they weren't.

Vive: Here's another listener question. It's Fernando from Lima, Peru. [01:28] He asks: "I am amazed that the different insects could communicate so well. Was this because they were getting smarter?"

Narrant: I know humans have studied pheromones and insect communication for decades, but your scientists only saw the tip of the iceberg. Our pheromones do so much more than sound alarms and attract mates. They are our nouns, verbs, expressions, and emotions and allow communication between ants and other insects. They are as complex as any human exchange. [02:02] These interactions existed at a basic level on Earth even before we arrived on Poo-ponic.

Vive: Narrant, that explains a lot. We humans don't give other species, especially insects, that much credit. Amazingly, Antuna's family maintained the records of the first colonists for mega-hexs. How is that even possible?

Narrant: As a historian and an ANT, I can tell you that ants are meticulous and have remarkable memories. But it was a concerted effort to pass accurate information from generation to generation. [02:35]

Vive: Incredible.

Narrant: I found stories of various descendants from different periods after insects made written records and diaries. The overlapping parts of the Antuna story were almost identical, so I am confident the tale is entirely accurate. It's our ancient history, but it is told precisely.

Vive: Although it was a long-kept history, Antuna's story was very poignant and impactful.

Narrant: Yes, it is almost like your Bible stories for us.

Vive: I can see that—she was brought back to life after her heart stopped, [02:59] became a mother in a way that was not traditional, and inspired insects to care about each other. She sounds like some of our prophets and saints.

Narrant: Of course, she was not perfect, but in time, insects idolized her, and most insects revere those that keep her story. Antunites not only remember her account but also try to live their lives reflecting Antuna's ideals.

Vive: I have one more question for you from a listener. It's from fourteen-year-old Heidi in Innsbruck, Austria. She says: [03:32] "I was so upset that the young friends died in your story, but I have learned from my history class that many innocent people die in war. I guess it is the same with insects, but I didn't realize that insects had evil leaders that start wars for revenge and to wield power."

Narrant: Yes, Heidi, insects have powerful instincts that drive revenge and the need to rule others, just like some human leaders. Your ancestors probably know this best of all, being at the center of two world wars. [04:00] Like humans, common insects are easy to fool and follow their leaders, often without question.

Vive: But it was so tragic that Antuna and her friends died.

Narrant: As your people say: 'war is hell.' There are many examples where humans died in wars or at the hands of those who oppress them.

Vive: I am ashamed to say we have too many examples to name them.

Narrant: But we all must remember them, learn from our past mistakes, and ensure not to repeat them. [04:32]

Vive: Indeed.

Narrant: A President of the United States of America,

Dwight Eisenhower, once said: "I hate war as only a soldier who has lived it can, only as one who has seen its brutality, its futility, its stupidity." His words remind me of the poignant words of Beefirst after she learned of Antuna's death: "No deeds can console the sorrows and depression, brought on by the arrows of aggression. And the largest price of war is paid by our youth. Through the loss of innocence, stolen by distortions of honor and truth." [05:00]

The End

APPENDICES

APPENDIX 1

Insect time units using heximal counting system as compared to human time

Insects count using a heximal system (i.e., base 6), and insect time reflects this counting. One hex is approximately equivalent to an Earth year and reflects one orbit of Poo-ponic around its solar star. Other time units use hex as a base and endings similar to a decade, century, and millennium. Except the rise is based on the power of 6 rather than 10. Thus, six times a hex is a hexade, 6X6 or 36 times a hex is a hexury, and 6X6X6 or 216 times a hex is a hexennium. Similar terms are used for months, weeks and days; except that a hexth is one-sixth of a year (about two months), a hexek is one-sixth of a hexth (or about ten days), and a hexay is one-sixth of a hexek (or 10/6 days = 40 hours). The terms hex-hexay (1/6 hexay), hexour, hex-hexour (1/6 hexour), hexute, hexond, and hex-hexond (1/6 hexond) are roughly equivalent to 6.67 hours, 1.1 hours, 11 minutes, 1.8 minutes, 18 seconds, and 3 seconds in human time.

Appendix 2

Pheromonic-English dictionary of insect emotions/non-verbal speech

abashing aroma: humiliation

abrasive aroma: annoyance

achy aroma: regret

acidic aroma: sarcasm

acrid aroma: hatred

affable aroma: contentedness

airy aroma: carefree

alluring aroma: attractive, sexy

anorexic aroma: saying nothing

antsy aroma: disturbed

appalling aroma: cruel

azure aroma: sad

babbling bouquet: gossipy

baked bouquet: conviction

ballooning bouquet: egotism

balmy bouquet: positivity

beaming bouquet: admiration

beefy bouquet: resistance

biting bouquet: sarcasm

bitter bouquet: ill-will, badness

blaring bouquet: angry crowd noise

blazing bouquet: hatred

blinding bouquet: overwhelmed

blistering bouquet: very upset

bloated bouquet: intense pride

blubbery bouquet: big lie, bold lie

blustery bouquet: argumentative
bold bouquet: defiance
booming bouquet: yelling
bouncy bouquet: excitement, happy
brassy bouquet: arrogance
brawny bouquet: strength
breezy bouquet: cheerfulness
bright bouquet: happiness
brilliant bouquet: optimism
brisk bouquet: petulance, crabbiness
bristly bouquet: grumpy, cranky
broad bouquet: confidence
broken bouquet: verklempt
bubbly bouquet: excitement, happy
buffed bouquet: strength, leadership
bulged bouquet: gratified, proud
bulky bouquet: hardy, resilient
buoyant bouquet: optimism
burly bouquet: overzealous
buxom bouquet: greedy
earthy essence: grounded
eased essence: targeted speech
echoing essence: stuttering
effervescent essence: optimism
electrifying essence: excited crowd
engorged essence: yelling by a crowd
enticing essence: alluring
explosive essence: deafening noise
delicate fragrance: soft voice
dim perfume: uncertainty
fat fragrance: obvious message

feathery fragrance: whisper
festal fragrance: merriment
festive fragrance: cheer, optimism
fiery fragrance: anger
firm fragrance: confidence
fishy fragrance: mysterious, devious
fizzing fragrance: uncertainty
flabby fragrance: stretch the truth
flaky fragrance: desperation
flapping fragrance: uncertainty
flashy fragrance: optimism, flare
flat fragrance: no emotion, monotone
flickering fragrance: idea
flimsy fragrance: fragile, weak
flowing fragrance: verbose, talkative
fluffy fragrance: gratefulness
fluttering fragrance: nervousness
foggy fragrance: confusion
foul fragrance: rotten, obscene
fragile fragrance: soft speech
freezing fragrance: fear
fresh fragrance: naïve, truthful
frigid fragrance: cold message
frosty fragrance: cold, unfeeling
fluid fragrance: articulate
fuming fragrance: angry
funky fragrance: strange
fuzzy fragrance: uncertainty
icy incense: cold fear
indigo incense: depression
inflamed incense: anger

inflated incense: egotism

intense incense: tension

intense perfume: insistence

ion-charged incense: excitement

itchy incense: eager, anxiety

odious odor: revolting

ominous odor: menacing

onerous odor: burdensome

padded perfume: guarded speech

pale perfume: soft speech

pealing perfume: screaming

piercing perfume: sudden loud noise

plaintive perfume: pleading speech

pleasant aroma: thrilled, happy

pleasant scent: sociable

plump perfume: arrogance, haughty

poignant perfume: dejected

pointed perfume: coherent message

polished perfume: eloquent speech

popping perfume: inspiration

portly perfume: pompous

prickly perfume: bristling speech

pudgy perfume: pushy

puffy perfume: pride

pulsating perfume: fearful

pungent perfume: irritation

puttering perfume: mumbling

radiant bouquet: enthusiastic

radiant reek: overjoyed, proud

ragged reek: cranky, disheveled

raging reek: anger

rambling reek: gossip

rasping reek: needling speech

ratty reek: annoyed

raw reek: naivety

rickety reek: anxiety, nervousness

ringing reek: scream

ripe reek: wisdom

roaring reek: loud, boisterous

robust reek: captivating

rocky reek: hard message

ruffled reek: panic

rumpled reek: alarm, terror

rutted reek: cringing, uncertainty

sapphire scent: sad

sapphire smell: gloomy

sapphire stench: suicidal

sapphire stink: depression

scalding scent: anger

scalding stench: evil, intense anger

scalding stink: angry response

scorching scent: hatred

scorching smell: anger, hatred

scorching stench: burning anger

scratchy stink: annoyed

scrawny scent: meek, guilty

screaming scent: obvious message

screaming smell: urgency

screaming stench: obvious deceit

screeching smell: urgent talk

screeching stink: urgency

scruffy scent: disheveled

searing scent: anger
seasoned scent: wisdom
seasoned smell: well-developed idea
seasoned stench: evil plan
seasoned stink: devious plan
secretive scent: whisper
seething stench: anger
seething stink: rage
shabby scent: upset
shabby smell: distressed
shabby stench: panicked
shabby stink: desperate
shadowy stench: deceit
shaky scent: uncertain
sharp scent: come back, rebuff
sharp smell: panic
sharp stink: sarcasm
shifty smell: deviousness
shifty stink: scheming
shimmering scent: happiness
shimmering smell: overjoyed
shimmering stink: ecstatic
shining scent: joy, contentment
shiny scent: happiness, joy
shiny smell: pride for others
shocking scent: surprise
shrill smell: alarming talk
shrill stink: alarmed
silken scent: smarmy
silky scent: romantic speech
sinewy scent: tough talk

sizzling scent: sexy

sizzling stench: anger, hatred

skinny, slim scent: shy

skinny, slim smell: cautious

skinny, slim stench: wary

skinny, slim stink: vigilant

slender scent: submissive

slender smell: gentle

slender stench: acquiescence

slender stink: compliance

slight scent: whisper

slimy scent: an obvious lie

slimy stench: deceitful plan

sludgy scent: unsure

smarmy scent: pleading

smarmy smell: beseeching

smarmy stink: evil plan

smooth scent: reassurance

smothering scent: frustrated, trapped

smoldering scent: passion

smoldering stench: lasting deceit

smoldering stink: growing deceit

sneaky stink: devious plan

snug scent: friendly

soft scent: caring speech

soggy scent: disinterested

soggy smell: unsure

solid scent: simple message

solid smell: rule

solid stench: evil rule

solid stink: unfair rule

soothing scent: reassurance
sour scent: resentful, bitter
sour stench: hostile
sour stink: sullen
sparkling scent: pride, joyfulness
sparkly scent: excitement
spiky scent: scheming
spiky smell: deceitful scheme
spiky stench: evil scheme
spiky stink: devious scheme
spindly scent: embarrassed, humbled
spiny scent: bullying
spiny smell: offensive
spiny stench: evil
spiny stink: cruel
sprightly scent: happiness
sprightly stench: ecstatic
squeaking stink: bothersome
squealing scent: screaming
stabbing stink: harsh insult
stale scent: dull, boring
stale smell: tedious
stalwart scent: brave
stanch scent: confidence
stanch smell: authoritative
steadfast scent: conviction
steamy scent: passion, sexy
steely stench: hard advice
steely stink: insistence
sticky scent: worry
sticky smell: anxiety, worried

sticky stench: devious
sticky stench: trickery
sticky stink: deception
stifling scent: oppression
stifling stench: overbearing
stinging scent: insult
stinging stench: sarcasm
stinging stink: insult
stirring scent: energized
stocky scent: unconvinced
stout scent: honest
stout smell: frank
stout stench: moral superiority
strangling stink: deep oppression
strapping scent: defiance
strapping stench: rebellious
stringy scent: tough talk
strong fragrance: pride
stroppy smell: awkward, obstinate
stroppy stink: belligerent
stuffy scent: arrogance
stuffy smell: conceit
suffocating scent: worries, anxiety
suffocating stink: cringeworthy
sulking smell: brooding
sultry scent: sexy
sunny scent: cheerful
sunny smell: overjoyed
sunny stench: ecstatic
sweet scent: nice
sweet smell: enjoyment

sweet stench: greedy
sweet stink: overindulgent
sweltering stink/stench: domineering
swollen scent: pride
swollen stench: megalomaniacal
syrupy scent: sentimental
syrupy smell: tricky
syrupy stench: devious
syrupy stink: cunning
thorny stink: devious scheme
vague vapor: uncertainty, hesitation
vacillating vapor: unsure, frightened
vexing vapor: confusion, upset
vibrant bouquet: proud
vibrant scent: ecstatic
vibrating vapor: trembling
vigorous reek: with authority
vigorous vapor: energized
vile vapor: evil
vinegary aroma: acidy smell
vinegary vapor: sarcasm
viscid vapor: sticky feeling
vivacious vapor: lively, excited
volatile vapor: aggression
waffling whiff: uncertainty
wafting whiff: uncertainty
wailing whiff: soft cry
warm whiff: tenderness, hope
wee whiff: whisper, quiet talk
wet whiff: rebuff
whining whiff: complaining

whispering whiff: subtle

wispy whiff: whisper

whistling whiff: brief shrill speech

wily whiff: cunning, tricky

withered whiff: muttering

APPENDIX 3

Quotations from Famous Persons and References to Movies, Books or Indigenous Lore

p. 14 "Wow, Beebie, I got a feeling we're not in Laramidia anymore!" From the movie 'Wizard of Oz,' where Dorothy says: "Toto, I've a feeling we're not in Kansas anymore."

p.16 "shaken but not overly stirred." From Ian Fleming's 'Dr. No,' "shaken and not stirred."

p. 43 Indeed, one could say they toiled and troubled till their soil was overturned and many times doubled. Reference to William Shakespeare's Macbeth: "Double, double toil and trouble."

p. 85 "I am afraid our planet is in great peril we can't belie, and if we keep carrying old grudges, we all will die." From Chief Seattle quote: "Our planet is in great trouble and if we keep carrying old grudges and do not work together, we will all die."

p. 119 "The most beautiful thing is the mysterious—to solve and know it can make you delirious." From an Albert Einstein quote: "The most beautiful thing we can experience is the mysterious."

p. 119 "Look deep into nature, both the spirit and letter, and then you will know it all so much better." From an Albert Einstein quote: "Look deep into nature, and then you will understand everything better."

p. 122 "Brilliant may be an *insect* botanist, but with war upon us, I am an *ant* scientist." From a Fritz Haber quote: "During peace time a scientist belongs to the World, but during wartime he belongs to his country."

p. 122 "Termite death is ant quell, lest we aim to inflict it well." From a Fritz Haber quote: "Death is death no matter how it is inflicted."

p. 127 "It is not what's right or the truth that matters, but a victory that puts termites in tatters." From an Adolph Hitler quote: "It is not truth that matters, but victory."

p. 128 "Our wars will not slow or have ceases until all spiders and termites rest in pieces." From an Adolph Hitler quote: "We shall only talk peace when we have won the war."

p. 131 "They have fed us a great lie to see danger where none exists. To mistrust our friends and treat strangers as cysts," Reference to the indigenous 'Story of the Peacemaker,' where Hiawatha is quoted: "We have all been fed a great lie, the lie of war. It makes us see danger where none exists; it causes us to distrust our friends, and to label the unknown as our enemy." As described in Mitchell, S. Sacred Instructions: Indigenous wisdom for living spirit-based change. North Atlantic Books, Berkeley, CA, 2018.

p. 137 "What luck for us insects who link that these termites don't plan or think." From an Adolph Hitler quote: "What luck for rulers that men do not think."

ACKNOWLEDGMENTS

The author wishes to acknowledge a few individuals who played a vital role in completing this novel. First, I want to thank my wife, Ann Birdgenaw, for I would not have written this book without her inspiration. She also played an essential role as a reading partner and proofreader. I also want to thank my book coach and developmental editor Nina Munteanu, a fellow author and scientist, and a creative writing instructor. Nina inspired me to expand my work from a novella to a trilogy, and her suggestions taught me the essentials of fiction writing. Additional thanks to the author and editor Erin Bledsoe, who helped with the finishing touches. Thanks to my kids, Kelly, Sophie, and Justin, for their encouragement and comments. Famous quotes or indigenous lore inspired many of the insect rhymes.

ABOUT THE AUTHOR

The author, Terry Birdgenaw, is a Metis of Oji-Cree, English, Scottish, Dutch and French-Canadian heritage, whose mother's first cousin is a long-time lead elder of the Metis Nation of Canada. However, Terry would argue that by moving away from the Oji-Cree territory a few generations ago, his family became assimilated by European Canadian culture. Yet, Terry has long been fascinated by the story of his ancestor, Mistigoose, the indigenous Canadian woman who was the first to welcome a European into his mother's family line.

Mistigoose was both a tragic figure and an inspiration for this novel and series. Her tragedy was that she drowned herself while distraught over the loss of her first son William, whom her British husband Robert had taken permanently to England. Against her will, the author's fifth great grandfather wanted to ensure their son would be eligible to receive a handsome inheritance promised to his heir. Ironically, as British law prohibited Metis from owning property, William never received his rightful inheritance, so his translocation and mother's death were both in vain.

The translation of Mistigoose, an Oji-Cree word, inspired parts of the story told in *The Antunites Chronicles*. In English, Mistigoose means little branch or twig. The title character of *Antuna's Story*, whose own mother drowned, used a twig in a selfless effort to save her newfound friend Dinomite. The resolution of the second book in the series, *The Rise and Fall of Antocracy*, also depended on the insectoids' realization that they needed tiny insects to break down little branches to generate the new soil required to rehabilitate their spent lands.

Visit Terry at:
TerryBirdgenaw.WordPress.com
https://twitter.com/TerryBirdgenaw
https://www.instagram.com/authorterrybirdgenaw/
https://www.facebook.com/TerryBirdgenawWriter

ABOUT THE SERIES

Antuna's Story is the first book in *The Antunite Chronicles*. It follows the lives of Earth insects transported through a wormhole to a far-off planet they call Poo-ponic. Young Antuna encouraged the settlers to work together, but hexs later, conflicts resumed. Despite her convictions, Antuna could not save herself or her diverse friends from the devastation of war. Still, surviving stories told how Antuna fought discrimination, saved the colony from starvation, reversed gender roles, became a scholar, and led the resistance effort. And though just a tiny ant, Antuna's actions changed society forever.

Look out soon for *The Rise and Fall of Antocracy*, the second book in *The Antunite Chronicles*. This *Animal Farm*-like story tracks the insects' evolution to cyborg insects, the growth and decline of a fledgling democracy, and the destruction of life on the planet caused by a long-ignored climate crisis. It also follows the utopian society created by a group of cyborg insects that escape to Poo-ponic's moon Bilaluna before Poo-ponic's atmosphere collapses.

The Antunite Chronicles' third book will be released later this year. The novel *Antunites Unite* begins a couple of generations after insectoids from Bilaluna recolonize their old planet with its rejuvenated atmosphere, which they rename Intopia. Despite their optimism, an authoritarian leader takes control of the colony and uses genetic manipulation to replace unwanted insect cyborgs and biological alterations and sociological rules to dominate its inhabitants. It is an allegory reminiscent of *1984* and *Brave New World,* where rebel spies must overcome a dystopian regime that uses histrionics, bionics, and socionics to subjugate its citizens. It's a brave new world that's out of this world!

www.ingramcontent.com/pod-product-compliance
Lightning Source LLC
Chambersburg PA
CBHW021147190726
48288CB00008B/2861